ALSO BY C.C. BERKE

Man, Kind

DESTINATION EARTH

TWENTY SHORT STORIES

WRITTEN BY:
C.C. BERKE

ILLUSTRATED BY:
BRENT PLOOSTER

SODAK
PUBLISHING

Published in the United States by Sodak Publishing, LLC.
www.sodakpublishing.com

Originally published in hardback in May of 2022

Hardback ISBN: 978-1-7362335-3-5
Paperback ISBN: 978-1-7362335-4-2 -or- 978-1-7362335-6-6
Ebook ISBN: 978-1-7362335-5-9 -or- 978-1-7362335-7-3

Cover Design and Illustrations by Brent Plooster
www.brentiisdesign.com

Interior Design by Christopher C. Berke
www.ccberke.com

Instagram: @ccberke
Twitter: @thechrisberke
Facebook: /ccberke
Goodreads: C.C. Berke

FIRST EDITION

For travelers.

CONTENTS

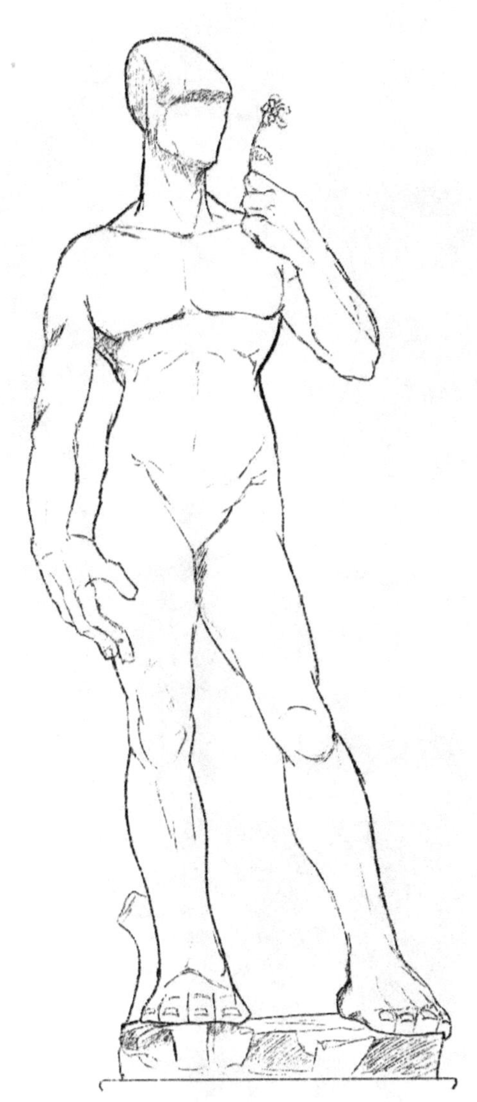

ÐESTINATION EÅRTH

PART I

Earth trembled again as the Didact led her council further down into the crust. What had once been humanity's nucleus for scientific advancement was now reduced to a snaking network of jagged caves. Caves where large stones perpetually shook themselves free and slammed into the paths, forcing the final reminders of an entire species to zig and zag with extreme heed. Still, they had to try. Mankind depended on it.

Briefly the quaking paused. The council used this fleeting stability to catch their feet and gain some lost ground.

"Is everyone here?" the Didact shouted without looking back. She thought she had heard all twelve reply, but could not risk precious moments counting heads. Every second was a gift.

The council reached the end of one rubble-lined hallway, then scrambled down another. Like the planet's slow, dying breaths, tremors continued to rise and fall with predictable malice. Danger and safety blended seamlessly into one constant—fear—but the group persevered until a dead end forced them into a makeshift tunnel illuminated by a string of flickering bulbs.

"We're almost there!" the Didact yelled as she squeezed in first, briefly noting how the gap had narrowed since her last entry. If they had fled just one hour later, it may have been closed for good.

One by one the council turned their bodies sideways and shimmied through the fissure as quickly as Earth would allow. Jutting rocks scraped into their chests and backs. As the last member entered, another rumble initiated a massive *crack!* that vibrated from deep within. The caves were shifting.

"Hurry!" the Didact pleaded as she popped out the far end. "I can see the light of the facility!"

She spun to pull outstretched arms from the closing aperture, each one with more friction than the last. *Eight . . . nine . . . ten . . . eleven.* Once she grabbed the hand of the last council member, Earth shook more violently than ever. The quake overwhelmed the Didact's grip and she fell flat on her back.

"Go on without me!" the trapped member pleaded.

"Save them!"

"We *need* everyone!" the Didact commanded, lurching back to her feet.

"No! Our time is up!"

The Didact knew it to be true, but emotion begged her to try. She reached for the final member's hand once again only to find it had retracted. "Go," its owner softly said.

Another deafening *crack!* was heard from high above and a hanging boulder shifted. Exposed, the risk would only grow for the final eleven, so the Didact withdrew and turned to run the last leg of the race for their lives.

Around the final corner the Didact and her council stumbled into the vibrating science facility. The enormous domed area appeared to be scooped directly from the rock and was vast enough for a small town to grow inside. But the once-pristine lab was now littered with scrapped machines, makeshift ceiling supports, mounds of loose sediment, and the occasional neglected corpse. At the center of the dome, towering hundreds of meters above them, was a gargantuan silver sphere seemingly suspended by the will of itself. Beneath the lustrous orb an incomprehensibly thick, intertwining network of cables connected it to a bottomless pit bored deep into the floor.

"Is it finished?" the Didact hailed when they all reached the foot of the sphere. Their necks craned up in awe at the impossible construct.

A scientist poked his head out from behind a holographic

computer and replied, "Nearly. Can we speak?"

"Wait here," the Didact asked of her council, then approached the scientist's glowing workstation. The tremors continued their rhythmic ups and downs, but only when she was certain they could not be overheard did she ask, "Can this thing really save our people? Give us a new life?"

The scientist stopped his frantic typing. "I thought you would bring twelve," he said, solemnly looking out at the scant remaining lives.

She hung her head. "We lost one in the caverns."

"This is not great news. How many have made it off the planet?"

"None," the Didact said, forcefully holding her composure. "Earth is imploding under our feet, swallowing up any form of escape we may have had. Your machine is our last hope."

The scientist glared back at the hologram, which seemed to periodically load different sorts of processes in the form of colored lights that were far beyond the Didact's understanding. "What would you sacrifice to save the human race?" he asked unexpectedly.

"This isn't the time for riddles!" the Didact snapped, allowing desperation to slip through her forbearance.

The scientist shook his head with a great weight. "Earth's surface has been uninhabitable for decades now. Because of the Resource Wars, water no longer flows, clouds no longer form, and green no longer shades. Centuries of pollution punctured our fragile ozone, amplifying radiation from both the sun and our bombs, forcing our civilization underground forever. Then, through no lessons learned, we continued to abuse what little we had left. Our great machines literally dug and drilled and mined this once-living planet to death. So," he pressured, "what would *you* sacrifice?"

The Didact reared, clearly never having considered this option. "Are you asking if we, if humanity, even deserves saving?"

The scientist respectfully nodded his head. "That is for you to decide, Didact."

She looked back at her council. Every single one of them stood on trembling legs and ground, fearful they would be the next to perish inside this crumbling world. *It's not their fault,* she beseeched herself, *And it's not mine either. Previous generations left us with this . . .*

The Didact returned her attention to the scientist. "What exactly does this thing do?"

"Our planet can no longer provide safety, nutrients, or life, but it *can* provide one final gift. It can give us a clean slate."

The Didact's ears perked. "That sounds perfect! How does it work?"

The scientist guided her back towards his workstation. "I have found another location among the cosmos that can sustain us, but this device has a certain set of . . . physics . . . it must abide by. We need this planet and, ironically, this planet still needs us. However, I cannot ameliorate one or the other. Not as is."

"Explain," the Didact said with annoyed urgency behind her voice.

"When I say 'clean slate', I mean starting over . . . from the *very* beginning." The scientist began pointing to various sections of the holographic version of the sphere. "My machine can only deconstruct matter down to its most finite particles and then reconstruct them on another plane. To accomplish that, it requires a monumental amount of power. Power which can only be obtained by harnessing the Earth's core. That means you, me, the council, all thirteen of us, will erupt from a single atom. *We* won't exist anymore, not as we are, but our planet, and the human race, will get a second chance."

"Are you insane?! We can't possib—"

Another quake shook the facility and the far side of the lab split and disappeared into the empty Earth. Tiles and machinery severed from the walls, landing with explosions of dust and shrapnel. The entire floor shifted as the scientist lunged for the Didact and grabbed her shoulders. "Look around! There is no *insane* anymore. Only action. Either we all die here today, for good, or we begin anew somewhere else. But the decision *has* to be now!"

Suddenly, a peak from a nearby mountain crashed through the domed ceiling, creating a rift in the protective rock above. Scorching sunlight punched through the opening and set fire to a wayward corpse. The scientist stumbled to the ground and the Didact jumped back in terror. Witnessing the violence of the flames brought a painful reminder of what their ancestors had done to their beautiful, generous planet. A planet that was now taking its revenge.

She stole one more poignant glance at her council. *We're still so young,* she thought as the eleven clutched each other in deep embrace. None of them had ever lived above the surface, felt the rains fall, watched the flowers bloom. She closed her eyes. *I know we can do better. Even if it's not. . .us.*

Finally the Didact heaved the scientist to his feet and looked at him through teary eyes. Eyes wise beyond their youth. Eyes that should never have gazed upon these horrors. "Do it."

Without a moment to spare, the scientist fled back to the holographic computer. He typed in commands that switched the sphere's flickering display from red to green. Then a new tremble began. Not a viscous, sporadic tremble, but the smooth, deep thrum of a powerful machine. Then things got louder, and brighter, and less tangent.

The last thing the Didact heard was the scientist assuring her, "Tomorrow will be better."

THIS AMERICAN LIFE

"Good morning!" hails a buoyant voice from the boundless void that was once non-existence. Curiously, you understand it, though you've never heard a voice. Much less a sound. "Due to your skin color, physical stature, and mental cognition, you've been preselected for a life of labor!"

Something is beneath you. It's hard and textured. And other hard things are connected to you, plugged into you, holding you in place. Another sound makes its presence. Not like the voice. This one clangs then whirs then thrums. You begin to move, but not of your will.

Everything is dark.

No, wait, something emerges from within that darkness.

It approaches you. Your eyes understand, but your brain does not. The affirmative voice speaks from it.

"Since you're not very productive at birth, We thought We'd go ahead and speed up the aging process by injecting a proprietary formula of chemicals unknown to you! Isn't that something?"

Warm fluid tunnels through your veins and you sense growth. Bones. Muscles. Comprehension. It feels good. Then a thought inaugurates...a question...your first question...but the fluid turns frigid and strikes it down. It feels like you've been bitten. It feels bad.

"You're probably wondering just how the heck you can understand me, huh? Don't panic! We've found that by introducing basic language prior to consciousness We cut down on time-to-maturity by twenty-eight percent. That means you and I can be best friends as soon as you open your eyes. Efficiency is fun!"

The object speaking to you now takes shape in your mind. A square . . . no . . . a box . . . no . . . a television. It hovers at eye level. Lingers. A face from within the screen smiles statically and around its edges many dials and lights and indicators tick and flash. You're not sure why, but you're attracted to televisions. Like some thing to some element, though a slight stab of cold disallows this interpretation.

"While that formula does its business," the static smile resumes, juddering ever so slightly, "why don't we begin the Controlled Risk and Sanctioned Habits education program?

Or, as We like to call it, the C.R.A.S.H. Course! Isn't that clever? All you have to do is keep your eyes on me while I teach you how to become a valued and productive citizen!"

The smile in front of you judders again and fades. Something new fills its place. A shape.

"This is a box," says the voice, still existing from within the television. "You'll be assembling countless numbers of these during your calculated lifetime of seventy-eight years."

Continuing in sequence is a cylinder, then a tube, then a tray, and so forth. Following shapes become more abstract. There is a unique shape called a tape dispenser. One called a barcode scanner. One called a retractable utility knife. Another called a conveyor belt. You look down at the hard, textured thing ushering you forward and begin to understand. The cold returns to your veins to remove any conclusions you may have been drawing.

"And now we'll move on to colors!" the television exclaims, changing its screen to a solid hue of some sort. "This is green and it generally means to go, or to continue. This one is red. It generally means to stop, or that it's time for your mandatory ten-minute replenishment break. Don't forget your Aliment!"

After you've been shown all ten colors and their general implications, the television announces that you're ready to combine shapes and shades to identify living things. Something brown and sleek and small appears on the television and though you can't explain it, you're certain that it's dead.

"Animals, or as We designate them, pests, are viewed as unnecessary and should immediately be eliminated before they disrupt our supply chain. Rats like these chew through equipment and carry diseases. Gross!"

A slightly larger grey animal with black around its eyes replaces the rat. Also dead.

"Raccoons rifle through our waste and carry diseases."

The slideshow of lamented wildlife continues.

"Birds excrete from above and carry diseases. Insects contaminate our food and carry diseases. Dogs serve only as distractions and carry diseases. Cats offer no value whatsoever and also carry diseases. A fun motto we have around here is that, 'If it has more legs than two, it should be killed by you!'"

One insect that had appeared on screen was named a moth. This flying animal is attracted to fluorescent high bay lights much in the same way you are attracted to this television. The glow and hum coming from a singular location calms both you and it. A thought from before returns and solidifies. *Like a moth to a flame* reaches your cortex, then is bitten away by icy teeth.

The static smile returns.

"Let's move on to mathematics. This subject can be challenging for some, but don't worry. We can reinforce any shortcomings while We're still plugged directly into that ol' gourd of yours. Ha! Isn't that funny? I just referred to your brain as a gourd. That's called a metaphor!"

A grouping of four numbers takes the smile's place on the screen and the voice tells you about your schedule. Currently it's eight in the morning, you were animated at seven, and the other two to remember are nine and five. You are treated with some reinforcing warmth before moving on to what's called simple arithmetic.

"Now, if I have four-hundred packages that must ship by five o'clock, and only two-hundred packages are completed as of two o'clock, how many packages are still needed to fulfill this order, and how much time do I have to fulfill it?"

Synapses in your brain absorb the question and attempt to connect conclusions with naive neurons. Numbers start to form behind your eyes, but they are best described as fuzzy. The answer is blurred to you until another shot of warmth massages your brain and reveals the solution with sharp precision.

"Very good!" congratulates the television's smile, somehow knowing you have arrived at the answer before you speak it. "You're a natural!"

Suddenly, the conveyor belt ushering you along the emptiness comes to a silent halt. Whatever various things that were attached to you release and you stand for the first time under your own mind and muscle. A metallic hand clamps your left forearm and raises it to strap a device around your wrist. You look at it and a smile similar to the one that's been educating you appears inside a smaller iteration of its screen.

"This is a PVT," the television's voice informs. "Your

Personal Vitality Tracker. This little doodad records everything from the amount of steps you take per day, to your heart rate, and all the way down to the oxygen level in your blood. How neat is that?"

The clamp releases your arm and you stare at the miniature television now attached permanently to you. There are various bars indicating progressions that you don't understand and a group of four numbers that you do understand. They read eight-forty-five.

"If your vital recordings ever deviate from normal, the PVT will escort you to the nearest Medical Booth where you will be injected with enough BioSeal to keep you upright and working for as long as possible. For free. What a bonus!"

An abrupt clanging noise follows your instructions and a horizontal bar of light makes itself known along the floor. It grows slowly upwards and you realize a door is opening.

"Congratulations!" The television says. "You have graduated from your C.R.A.S.H. Course. Sadly, this is where our friendship comes to an end. But don't worry, you'll meet lots of new friends soon enough!"

"Like me!" the small face around your wrist exclaims.

Laughter discharges like static from the larger's digital throat. "Ha. Ha. Exactly!"

The door is halfway open now, but the bright light of beyond is blinding. You lift a hand to shield your newborn eyes.

"One last thing," the hovering television directs.

Then its smile judders, fades, and is replaced with a short list of words that are read aloud to you at great speed. "Any use of 'We', or references to the greater 'We', are all trademarks of Sahara Industries. We are not liable for any misunderstandings, injuries, or mental stagnations resulting from the C.R.A.S.H. Course. We reserve the right to dispose of inefficient properties."

And with that the television and its friendly face disappears upwards into the blackness, leaving you at the edge of the conveyor looking out into a world brand new to you. There are buildings as far as your developing eyes can see. Smoke pours relentlessly upward out of each one. The sky has a tint of brown, a color you have only just learned matches that of pests and of death. The sun looks weak. Your education tells you these are factories. That they are important. Vital.

Before you is your future. Behind you is another buoyant, "Good morning!" Beneath you are green arrows painted in sequence on black concrete, silently directing you to the nearest building labeled "Boxing Facility". An alarm on your wrist starts beeping and you look at your PVT.

It's nine.

There is nothing warm or cold to signal your brain this time, but your first steps out into the new world automatically pull a smile across your face.

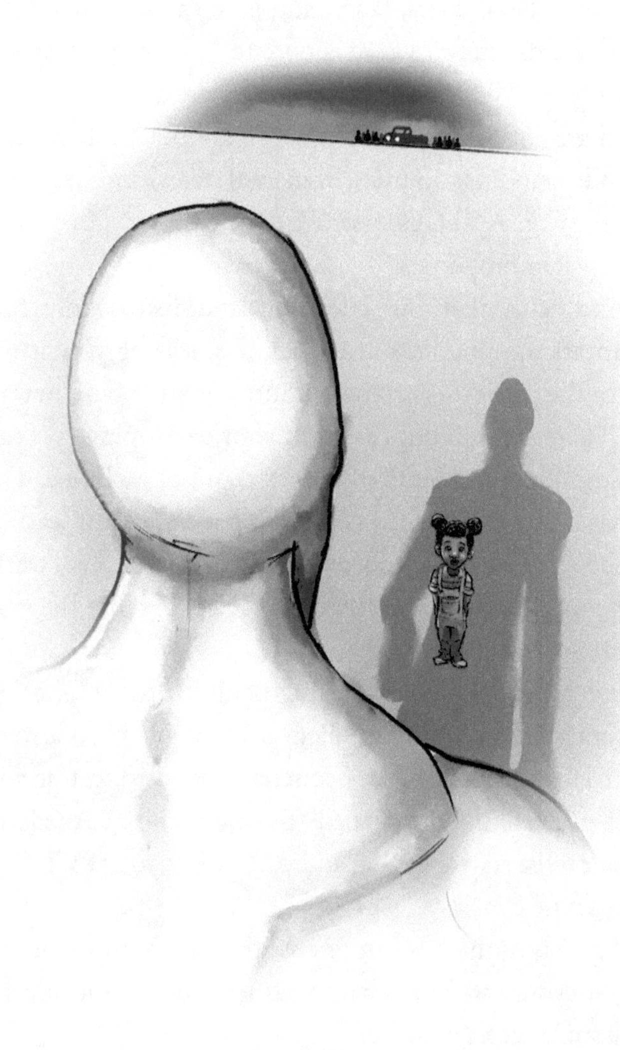

THE TRÅVELER

The intriguing thing about a modern technological revolution is that all of humanity was able to witness the Event in real time. The fact that we were capable of live-streaming something so gigantic, so pivotal to our species, from every angle, astounds me to this day. Camera-equipped drones from all corners of the globe flocked like migrating birds to provide a non-stop, twenty-four-hour feed to the masses. Citizens near Times Square forwent their daily commutes in favor of huddling beneath the hundred-foot screens, religious factions of all denominations prayed upwards for divine answers, and students (like myself at the time) found it overwhelmingly difficult to absorb the teachings of their professors. Suddenly new questions replaced old questions. Where is it from? Why is it here? What can we learn? And even though mankind can revisit the footage over and over and over again, I fear that we as humans may never be able to comprehend the Traveler's true purpose.

With such a grand occurrence witnessed by elite and amateur journalists the world over, I was astonished when Greenburg Magazine contracted me exclusively to write this exposé. A compliment no matter how daunting the task. The job description was clear-cut: compile dates, names, and standout occurrences into a rational narrative; something condensed and leisurely to put a tense society at ease. Easier said than done, mind you, and even though I spent months scouring the footage and assembling a comprehensive timeline, I never could discern a motive of any reliable nature. I'll just have to let this story speak for itself.

From what I can hypothesize, the Traveler, as we have come to name it, descended from the cosmos early in September of 2032 and claimed its stake at the center of a field in who-knows-where South Dakota (actually it was between Clark and De Smet). He, she, or it was humanoid in shape, yet lacked any of the defining reproductive organs one would consider male or female. It was impossibly tall, sixteen or seventeen feet, had Herculean musculature, and blindingly white . . . I'll say skin. On what we would consider a face were no imprinted features of any life form discovered on Earth. An ultimately smooth void inhabited the absence of eyes, nose, mouth, and expression. However, as you will read, that despite lacking these perceived evolutionary advantages, the Traveler had undoubtedly transcended any need for them.

September 15th, 2032 marked mankind's first recorded encounter with the Traveler. It was, for lack of a better phrase, embarrassing yet colorful. Three rural Dakotans had noticed a faint glow in the distance after turning down a back road following a night of festive drinking. Curiosity got the best of them and they decided to inspect. The old pickup truck took a small path through some harvest-ready corn and eventually pulled into a clearing. That's where this encounter begins. The recording came from a live, three-minute social media stream that dictates as follows:

A shaky-handed G-Phone captures a ghostly goliath squatting in the clearing of corn. It was mysteriously whisking away the crop (with the wave of a single hand) to create room for some sort of platform. (Researchers would later come to find that the Traveler had created a flawlessly smooth, flawlessly tempered glass surface from the ground below.) We then hear one of the three men from outside the frame shout, "Hey! What the hell do you think you're doing?" The gigantic being ignores the message and continues its excavation, which causes friction in the first man's blood-alcohol level. The cameraman swivels to the second of the men lowering the truck's tailgate to retrieve a shotgun. When the focus returns to the Traveler, one can spot the first man throwing (presumably) a beer can at the muscular back of the creature. It pauses, stands fully erect, and rotates its body to face the culprit. Heavy breathing picks up from behind the camera while plenty of expletives are picked up from in front. The tosser of the can begins to say, "That's right, I'm talking to—" but starts levitating and disappears from view. The second man with the shotgun pumps the fore-end and proceeds to take aim. I assure you what happened next was not a product of poor camera framing or lighting. At the end of the barrel, the expected explosion from gunpowder exits, freezes in midair, and is reversed back into the chest of the one who pulled the trigger. Immediately following, the camera fell to the ground and went black. None of the men were ever seen again.

It only took three hours after the Initial Contact Video was posted for the United States Army to make an appearance. Before the sun could shed its first light, a massive infantry migrated to that Midwestern corn field and surrounded the stage made of glass that the Traveler now stood upon. A four-star General by the name of Richard Greely addressed the alien from a PA system safely tucked behind some makeshift bulwark. The first thing Greely announced (as if a panel of pulp science-fiction enthusiasts hastily gave the briefing) was, "We come in peace." Above, four Lockheed Martin F-35 Lightning IV jets screamed through the air in a diamond formation. The Traveler remained unfazed. "By issue of the United States Government and on, um . . . " He stuttered. An opportunistic media-drone swooped in at the General's apprehension, pressuring him to continue. " . . . On behalf of planet Earth, we inquire about the purpose of your visit."

Still no answer. In fact, not even a shift of the weight on the Traveler's massive legs.

Hours went by (and you can look up the semi-hilarious transcripts yourself) while General Greely barked requests at the Traveler to no avail. The F-35 jets continued to circle in formation while tanks, Humvees, and a plethora of other military vehicles rearranged themselves for optimal advantage. From a media-drone's-eye-view, black SUV's came and went with manila folders like ants delivering dried leaves to the colony, then retreating to acquire more. Random frequencies were played through the PA system, symbols from ancient languages and universal equations were displayed on massive screens, and even the playlist from Voyager's Golden Record was presented to the Traveler without so much as a blink. (*Blink* is used here as an expression since the Traveler did not have eyes in any form that we could understand.)

Eventually the sun reached high noon and the U.S. Military ran out of space to cram any more war machines inside that crowded field. The F-35s circled back for what must have been the thirtieth flyby, only this time there was something different about the pass. From what was later revealed to be a sharp glare from the pristine glass terrace below, the right-flanking jet mistook the blinding flash as an aggression from the Traveler and dove straight down to attack. The rogue Lightning IV barrel-rolled with its Gatling gun armed and opened fire on the white giant. Instantaneously, the Traveler's left hand shot upwards and refracted the twenty-five millimeter bullets back towards their source. Metal shrapnel ate through the entire F-35 carapace like termites through a tree stump until what survived was a plane-shaped husk.

As the shell of the jet freefell towards the Traveler, something happened that had never been witnessed by human eyes prior. The F-35 had already reached terminal velocity so the Traveler's next moves could only be viewed by rewinding the feed and playing it back frame-by-frame. In one frame the Traveler clenched its fist. In the next the jet had disappeared completely. Then it was clear by some reflection of the sun that the plane-husk had somehow crystallized into glass (just like the land below the Traveler's feet). Finally, the Traveler's arm returned to its side and all that reached the ground was a whisper of ultrafine dust. Nothing remained of the Lightning IV or its pilot.

What followed was a mistake that mankind has made time and time again throughout the centuries. General Greely dropped the PA's handheld and picked up a satellite phone rushed over to him by his Private. The General spoke into it with conviction and nodded until whoever was on the other side produced a grin on Greely's face. He then tossed the phone back to the Private, who hastily retreated to an above-ground bunker, and reclaimed his handheld microphone. A few official orders later and every tank, jet, and missile launcher in the area took aim at the Traveler's heart (or whatever it was that sat behind its chest). Greely, hand raised high as an answer to his opponent's, clenched his fist and the battalion unleashed hell on Earth at the extraterrestrial.

After roughly thirty seconds of assault, the General called a ceasefire and waited for the smoke to clear. At first it appeared the Traveler had gone, that something replaced it, but it was uncertain what that something might be. In another thirty seconds it was clear that nothing had replaced the Traveler at all, only the space surrounding it. Every shard of every projectile that had been sent towards the white titan was now orbiting the being in its new glass form, just as with the jet. The crystalline sphere shimmered for a few silent moments, then evaporated away in an orb of more ultrafine dust. Finally, after yet another thirty seconds, the Traveler stretched its arms out as wide as they would go, transformed every object of war (including the humans) into glass, curled its fingers back in, and carpeted the field with a new layer of glistening topsoil. The retaliation was swift, silent, and (what we all hope, anyway), painless.

Months passed after more than a thousand men and women were reduced to shiny soot. Not a soul on this planet dared come into conflict with the Traveler from then on. Sure, scientists, world government officials, and foolish tourists would stop by from time-to-time to gawk, but the field remained barren and the titan remained still. The world settled back into its business just as it had before September 15, 2032. The Traveler became less of an intruder and more of a dark truth nestled in the back of everyone's minds; right between systemic racism and the ever-changing climate. In fact, most of Earth's population (myself included) shoehorned the Traveler into their daily routines. We would still make breakfast, scroll through social media, read emails, then casually check in on the unmoving intruder. For a while, memes, documentaries, articles, and large betting pools circulated around the Traveler, but even God himself grows cold when placed on the back burner.

—

Grass died, winds blew, snow fell, winter thawed, storms thundered, and, just as the first wildflowers of spring teased their colors, the world seized once again. On May 3rd, 2033, the Traveler moved.

An old white van emerged from the overgrown field and pulled right up to the glass platform. Out stepped a blue-robed man. Behind him were four other men in matching blue uniforms. They all paused at the edge of the glass, spoke to each other in a huddle, and then the robed one climbed onto the stage. Immediately, the Traveler turned to face him.

A media-drone dove to film the strange interloper as

he casually dropped his robe to his feet. The man's identity was suddenly revealed to the world as heavyweight boxing champion Sergio Popov. With twelve-ounce gloves already taped tightly around his fists, Popov was initiating possibly the most bizarre, yet fearless, publicity stunts of all time.

The boxer took one step forward and the Traveler mirrored him. Then Popov took another step. So did the Traveler. Step after step they approached each other, but one of them was making an additional movement. Just as astounding and frightening as the glass-to-dust ability, the Traveler could also change its size! So much so that when the boxer and the white giant reached each other, they were equal in height. Toe-to-toe the two paused. Another drone caught Popov swallowing anxiously, glancing back at his team, and, finally, raising his fists.

Like everyone else, I remember this bout like it happened this morning. Popov took his stance, bounced on the balls of his feet, and circled his opponent just as calculatingly as he would in the ring. Meanwhile, the Traveler swiveled on the inside (instinctively keeping square with the boxer). After a few fakes, Popov finally went for the Traveler's head with a lightning-fast, professional jab. A direct hit! I could hear cheers emanating from all over my apartment complex as Popov instantly catapulted to global icon status. There was another jab, then a cross, then a hook, then a few more jabs, and soon the entire world was screaming the boxer's name. Popov! Popov! Popov!

However, the celebration was short-lived. Not only did the power of Popov's fists have zero effect on the Traveler, but after four more strikes the cosmic being had somehow deciphered every movement the boxer had ever perfected. The Traveler squared up similarly to Popov and began dodging. Jab, miss. Hook, miss. Uppercut, miss. Cross, miss. No further stratagems came unexpected. Earth's champion would not land another punch in the iconic Popov v. Traveler matchup.

Mankind realized in unison the heartbreaking truth once the Traveler began counter-punching. So did Sergio Popov. A jab triple the speed of the world-class athlete's met Popov's temple. The boxer shook off the stunning pain and tossed another combination. Each strike was expertly and precisely sidestepped and was met with blows far stronger than any human could deliver. Seconds later, Popov was down. Viewers (myself included) were on the edge of their seats wondering if he, too, would go through the signature glass-to-dust transformation.

But nothing of the sort happened.

Fists still raised defensively, the Traveler patiently waited for the human to rise back up. Popov obliged, went another twenty seconds, then was promptly returned to his hands and knees. He could take no more. Realizing this, the Traveler lowered its own arms and paused calmly while the boxer lurched on the ground. It was minutes before Popov could find his breath. Once he did, he stood tall to face his opponent through bloodied brows and, just as in any professional match, he extended a glove in admiration. Briefly, the Traveler stood as frozen as it had since arrival. Then it unexpectedly reached its own hand out to benevolently meet the glove. The bedraggled boxer nodded, crossed the glass arena with head held high, and stepped off the most famous man in the entire world.

Bizarrely, Sergio Popov's success in not being reduced to a glimmering pile of dust came as a double-edged sword. It didn't take long for fighters from all around the world to appear in South Dakota so they too could try their hands at defeating the Traveler in combat. Masters of every discipline turned up in their formal outfits. Jiu-Jitsu, Greco-Roman wrestling, Judo, kickboxing, and even Taekwondo elites attempted to land that one perfect strike on the alien that would render it defeated. There was no such luck. Just as with boxing, the Traveler mastered every form of martial arts within seconds of studying its opponents. One-by-one they came, and one-by-one they left with bruises upon their bodies and tails between their legs.

Later that summer, mid-July to be precise, a Norwegian philosopher by the name of Lukas Bjelland surmised that perhaps the Traveler had not journeyed to Earth seeking that of a physical equal, but a psychological one. In an interview Bjelland went on to mention that, "a being of such insurmountable power has no need or desire for battle, yet may still yearn to be vindicated intellectually." Religious leaders boldly criticized the theories of Bjelland and publicly chastised him as a heretic. They established that there was no feasible way to understand the Traveler's intent since it was a "godlike" being sent from the heavens to extricate humanity. Naturally, the news media ran with the latter of the two voices on grounds that it was more controversial and, frankly, better for ratings. I'll note here that the media also failed to mention Bjelland's final statement on the matter (one I personally found most intriguing): that perhaps the Grandmaster from space merely, "came here to lose."

And speaking of Grandmasters . . .

In the wake of Lukas Bjelland's controversial theorem, top-tiered chess players began their own pilgrimage to South Dakota to trounce the Traveler in a battle of wits. The most notable was French Grandmaster Jeanne Laurent. She was the first to arrive and also carried the greatest statistical likelihood of success. She brought with her two folding chairs, a table, and a professional weighted chess set. As before, the Traveler turned to face her once she set foot upon the glass, approached as she got closer, and shrunk to match her size. Only when Laurent took her seat and extended her arm as an invitation to join did the Traveler effortlessly squat onto the chair (I say squat, but it was more like an aerial approach).

Jeanne Laurent, including her global audience, assumed the Traveler had never seen nor played anything remotely similar to chess. Piece-by-piece she meticulously placed the blacks on the far side of the board, followed by the whites on her side. Then she briefly paused to see if the Traveler would make a motion. It didn't. Next, with one flat hand raised to her opponent in the "stop" position, Laurent grabbed a pawn, mimicked its allowed movements, then returned the piece to its home.

Laurent emulated all fifteen movements until she finally grabbed the king. In contrast to the Queen, she moved it only one space in each direction, then held it up at eye level. The Traveler watched motionless. "This is the endgame," she said aloud. "The one piece you must protect while striving to topple your opponent's." To drive the point home, she placed the wooden king back down at the center of the board and, with her index finger, flicked it over. "Got it?"

Once all the pieces were back in their starting positions, Laurent (being the white side) went first. She moved a pawn forward one space and waited. The Traveler waited, too. Nearly ten minutes passed. Then another ten. And another. Laurent almost considered packing up when her opponent methodically reached over, grabbed a knight, and placed it in front of the wall of black pawns. The Grandmaster grinned.

Going forward the Traveler's pause between turns reduced significantly—from twenty minutes to ten minutes to one minute to nearly instantaneous counter-moves. Laurent went from being the shoo-in to on the run. Pieces were traded, queens were pulled out early, and strategies bloomed. Grandmasters study this monumental game even to this day. Some say that the start of Laurent's downfall was a brief moment of arrogance when the Traveler used its king offensively; that she had disregarded it as an amateur mistake. Others say she played the perfect game and that the Traveler set her up ten moves prior using a combination that had never been seen in chess before. Either way, Jeanne Laurent accepted her loss when her opponent slid a black rook to B9 and returned its hands to its lap. She momentarily stared at the board and then, with a smirk, flicked the white king over.

For the remainder of that summer the Traveler became more of a carnival attraction and less of a cosmic entity. Assuming that the titan was harmless if left unprovoked, countless professionals and hobbyists stood in line to try their hands at outsmarting the being. When classic chess grew hopeless, speed chess came in. Then it was checkers, Shogi, Stratego, Mahjong, Othello, and even Fencing. Any challenge that could be considered "intellectual" by the masses made its way onto that glass stage. Predictably, they all came, they all taught, and they all lost.

———

Nearly a decade passed and forgotten was a time when the Traveler turned an entire battalion into dust. Forgotten was the time it outranked our greatest martial artists in less than a three-minute round. And forgotten were the feeble attempts at besting the transient being in contests of mental strategy. Time moved on. We moved on. The field that housed the stage of glass moved on as well, regrowing lush wild grasses, shrubs, and flowers. Curious animals returned and skittered and played. Occasionally, a media-drone would catch a rodent scurrying across its feet, or a bird perching on its shoulder, but the Traveler prevailed; petrified in its own quandary of space and time.

It wasn't until August 23rd, 2041 that someone piqued the Traveler's interest for the final time. I had just handed in my thesis on *Sentient Life and its Motivations* (which, come to think of it, is probably how I got this gig), when I caught a live feed over lunch at the student union. At first we all thought a media-drone was on the fritz, recording a tuft of tall wild grass shuffling in the wind, until a young girl (now famously recognized as Mika Drew) popped out into the clearing and climbed up onto the glass. She was carrying a colorful box under her arm. The Traveler promptly took notice, approached her, and matched her small size.

Every single person in my vicinity dropped their utensils and trays and hurried over to the screens displaying the feed. "Turn it up!" someone yelled. I had reached the murmuration of students and staff just in time to watch five-year-old Mika sit cross-legged on the platform. She had already dumped the box out onto the pristine floor and started arranging its contents. The Traveler joined her.

Mika held out four bulbous plastic items (one red, one blue, one green, and one purple) for the Traveler to choose from, but it sat motionless. The girl grew playfully impatient after less than a minute's wait and picked her own color—green—and placed it on a sheet of paper between them. Then she lifted the remaining three baubles to the cross-legged humanoid opposite her and it gently selected purple. "Good choice," the media-drone recorded the girl saying. "Now hold on." She began organizing the rest of the small yellow pieces across the paper and started pointing profusely at different images.

"Is this some kind of toy?" I asked a nearby fellow student that had her G-Phone out. "You've never played this?" she scoffed. "It's called Cootie Bug." I shrugged while reaching into my own pocket so I could look up this foreign-to-me game. *Rules to Cootie Bug* I typed into a search field on my own G-Phone and then tapped the first result. In short, the game consists of assembling one's own Cootie Bug by rolling dice numbers equal to a corresponding body part. There is one body, one head, two antennae, two eyes, one tongue, and six legs. Rolling a one matches to the body, which is the first piece needed to continue. Next the player needs to roll a two for the head. Once the player has those initial two parts, the rest of the pieces and their corresponding numbers are fair game. The winner is the first to complete the anatomy of their Cootie Bug.

The young girl rolled to see who would go first, a four, then handed over the die, signaling the Traveler to do the same. Six. "Dammit!" a guy in my huddle shouted. Some chuckled, but most of us kept our gaze fixated on the screen. The girl handed over the die and then pointed again at the sheet between them that contained the legend of limbs. After a moment's pause, the Traveler let the die fall from its hand and it landed with a three facing up. "No good," Mika iterated, then she scooped the die back up for herself, tossed it between them, and leaned over to read the results: one.

A surprising murmur of encouragement came from the jumble of lunch-goers around me. Everyone began leaning into the game as if Cootie Bug was a craps table in Las Vegas. Now, with a green Cootie torso in hand, the girl rolled for the head: three. A wave of groans washed around me as she handed the die back to the Traveler. The pale opponent dropped the die again, landed a one, then collected its purple Cootie torso. Then it rolled again, a two this time, and seized the Cootie's head. Then again it rolled another two. Turn over. And with that, planet Earth had its first fair shot.

Back and forth Mika and the Traveler went, dropping dice and assembling their Cootie Bugs. At one point the Traveler had all six legs, but no eyes, tongue, or antennae, while the girl had the exact opposite plus one leg. She went on to roll a six to claim an additional leg, then the Traveler rolled another two, which forced another turnover.

The energy in the student union rumbled like a cloud filled with static! Passersby suddenly became cheering, booing, screaming, and groaning fans of Mika Drew. Some held wads of money in the air as betting fuel. Even I couldn't help but join in on the electricity with a few dollars of my own! I mean, at the time, no one could have guessed that what would unfold could only be described as an inconceivable stroke of cosmic luck.

The Traveler had amassed six legs, two eyes, and two antennae, but was still missing a tongue. Mika had only three legs remaining. It was the Traveler's turn and it had blown its roll on yet another two. The girl playfully picked up the die and effortlessly dropped a six. The student union released a thundering boom. She plugged a hole with a yellow plastic limb and rolled again: another six. Every single one of us lost our minds dancing around until Mika had the fifth leg inserted in her Cootie. Then she readied herself for one final roll. We all shushed each other until the union fell utterly silent. Wide-eyed, we watched the young girl sift the die around in her palm, blow on it with a missing-tooth smile, and release the white cube onto the smooth glass surface...

A six.

The ground beneath me shook with the celebration of eight billion humans jumping up and down at the same time. The girl who had scoffed at me earlier kissed me warmly on the lips, thawing me out as I stood frozen in disbelief. Students, faculty, and strangers were hugging, cheering, and calling loved ones to tell them . . . tell them . . . tell them what, exactly?

"Quiet!" someone shouted. "Something's happening!" We all paused and gazed at what followed on screen without so much as a breath. As Mika trotted her completed Cootie Bug around in a circle, the Traveler returned to full-form (as we have come to reference it), all seventeen feet of it. That was enough to pull the five-year-old's attention away from her toy. She rose from her knees, mouth wide open in amazement. The ethereal titan stood there in a slightly new position. Instead of impeccable, straight-up-and-down posture, the Traveler's head tilted forward towards the small girl and cocked slightly to one side, as if it was studying her . . . *admiring* her. Shortly after, the girl chuckled and slung her arms around the giant's leg with the affection a child gives to a doting parent. Once she released, the Traveler gently placed its massive hand on top of her fragile head, nodded, then began its ascent.

———

Eight years, eleven months, and eight days. That's how long the Traveler graced, or cursed, the surface of our planet. If three drunk Midwesterners had never discovered the giant humanoid poised on a platform of perfect glass in the middle of nowhere, it may very well still be standing there to this day. Now, only the platform remains and there's a new figure that stands upon it. Just as unmoving as its predecessor, a glass statue of Mika Drew occupies that flourishing field in remembrance of that fateful day.

I can safely say humanity changed after the Traveler.

Suddenly understanding that we were no longer alone in the universe burdened us with unstudiable existential questions for the rest of our lives. Are we the first? What's special about Earth? Will there be more? The answers are just as endless as the queries. None of us can presume why this transcendent being journeyed the cosmos to visit our small planet at the edge of the Milky Way Galaxy. Maybe the white giant came to survey our planet's defenses so it could return for our resources. Maybe, as Lukas Bjelland had theorized, the featureless titan was in search of a competition in which it could be bested. Or maybe—just maybe—the Traveler's sole purpose was to play the universe's most extraordinary game of Cootie Bug with a young South Dakotan girl named Mika Drew.

Prove me wrong.

THE NIGHT SHIFT

The first thing normies ask me is what it feels like. Always. My mind keeps going back to lice day in grade school. You know, when that nice lady ran the stick through your hair and every follicle on your body tingled? It's kind of like that. Or maybe it's closer to when someone unexpected whispers in your ear. Or when all your pores can't stop giggling while an ice cube slides down your spine. Either way, it's pretty much over as soon as it begins.

The next thing they ask is why I'm not constantly robbing banks or convenience stores. I politely reply that I'm just your run-of-the-mill shapeshifter, not fucking Mystique! There's no super strength or heightened senses coursing through my veins. I'm plain old skin and bone like anyone else. Besides, I appreciate living as much as the next girl. The thought of bullets whizzing by my head as I flee with a few hundred bucks of loose change is terrifying no matter who I look like.

Shortly after the standard bombardment of semi-harmless questioning, I've come to learn that normies tend to default back into being assholes. Especially the middle-aged white ones. They think I'm some all-powerful being that lurks in the darkness, waiting to steal their identities, and they don't stop to think about how much of that power actually belongs to them. More than I'll ever know. If anything, they're the ones that operate best in the shadows. In public they'll wave and smile and ask questions, but behind closed doors they swiftly pass laws to inhibit anything that's remotely different from them. Probably why most of us end up hanging ourselves before our mid-thirties.

When you're a kid shapeshifting seems like a blessing. You have all of these opportunities like sneaking into the boy's locker room, buying your underage friends their first beer, or, the jackpot, confusing the shit out of some unsuspecting twin. But even those shiny moments lose their luster over time. Sometimes you just want to use your "gift" to disappear from the face of the Earth for a while. In fact, most of the time that's all you want to do. At least I do.

Once I grew up the laws I mentioned before started following me like a damn shadow. NO shifting in public,

NO impersonating a public figure, NO using your ability for quote-unquote "malfeasance", and, well, you get the idea. Pretty much don't let the normies know who or what you are if you can help it and everyone can go on living in peace.

As a result I spent years trying to figure out who I really was. The more times I changed, the harder it was to remember the original me. The *true* me. I tried to assimilate into society by working normie jobs, but when you can do what I can do they don't really scratch that fulfillment itch. One perk is that I can't really be found so I'll never have to pay bills, but I still need to eat, drink, and sleep in a warm bed, ya know? That's when I discovered something that could bring happiness to normies at the expense of my own. Sounds depressing, but hey, it made me rich.

Our dwindling circle calls it the Night Shift. Since a traditional career path is often too menial for a Shifter, we have to get creative with our gigs. The quick and easy money usually comes in the form of standing in for a normie while they go do something...questionable. To varying degrees, most just need to take a leave of absence from their jobs or their spouses. Once I sat in as this unsuspecting man's wife for nearly a week. Another time I spent a night posing as a grounded high schooler while the kid went to a party. One of the most common requests is breaking up with someone's significant other. That one's pretty dickish, but does have its perks if you're a bit horny at the same time.

Not surprisingly, though, the real money for Shifters

lies in prostitution. There are assholes out there with money beyond imagination that spend their lives dreaming of fucking that one person in highschool that rejected them decades ago. And they all pay insane amounts of cash to finally do it. It's almost always married men, too. They must feel like they missed out on something, or that they need to prove to the me-that's-not-really-me that they're worthy. Luckily for them, and myself, I'm practically untraceable after the deed has been done.

I only have three rules before I get started with one of these creeps: pay up front, always use protection, and get the hell out as soon as we're finished. From there it's relatively simple as long as I check my soul at the door. They show me a picture of the one-that-got-away, I shift into them, they fuck me, then they leave ten thousand dollars poorer. I can't say I don't feel absolutely gutted after a Shift, but money's money.

Which leads me to why I'm even telling you this sob story of my life from the back of a Greyhound to nowhere in the first place. Something happened this morning. Something that changed me. Like a switch deep down in my body had been flipped and a new source of light appeared. Clarity.

I've never been one to leave a trace, let alone write down my thoughts inside a journal, but while I was waiting for this bus to arrive I saw a tiny Moleskine notebook sitting on the shelf next to the M&M's I picked up. My plan is to leave this story on the seat and hopefully it finds its way to someone who needs it most. I'm sure as shit no activist, but maybe it can bring some change into the world.

So here's how it all went down:

Before the sun came up, and an hour after being manhandled by some Big Tech billionaire that had a thing for his younger sister, I exited the five-star hotel he owned with a healthy stack of a hundred hundreds weighing down my purse. And even though he was long gone—per the agreement—something in this particular pre-dawn air sent a shiver down my spine. This guy had been a little unusual, and not just because of the sister thing. It felt more like a shadow crowding the corner of my eye.

You don't hear about it often, but it happens to Shifters who get careless. Some will use a client's fetish as a form of insurance; others embarrassment. I think of it as a self-satisfying tip for going through all the trouble. However, you can't always control the ultra-rich. And today I *may* have left a billionaire's hotel suite looking a lot like his sister on a proverbial walk-of-shame just so the paparazzi could have something juicy to photograph.

Anyways, that shadow spotted me as soon as I spotted it and it began to follow me, as shadows do. I dipped into the nearest empty alley to make a quick shift back into my natural form before any normies could witness. But just as the tingling sensation subsided a demanding, "Hey you!" came from close behind.

I turned to find a man with a trench coat and a low-brimmed hat approaching me. Since the other end of the alley was a brick wall, I slid my hand into my purse and clutched a small knife resting next to my fresh stack of money. I was also certain ten thousand dollars smelled a lot like the reward the billionaire offered this pursuer to whack me. How convenient.

"You messed up, Shifter," the shrouded man said. His pace picked up and something held near his waist flashed against the dim alley light. A knife of his own. "Mr. Greenburg values his privacy."

At that point it didn't matter who I looked like; my jig was up. With these guys, "Sorry, I'll never do it again," doesn't quite cut it. He knew normies would hardly bat an eye if a Shifter bled out on the cold concrete. "Well, *it* must have been doing something shifty," they'd say as the news segment transitioned, chuckling at their own clever use of words. I'm sad to say it, but this man basically had a free pass to take my life...and my hard-earned stack of cash.

When he was within steps of me I prepared to pull out my own self-defense from my purse. Even the blackness of night had retreated behind the calm blue of dawn so as not to be considered an accomplice. The streetlamps faded. His footsteps echoed. My entire soul clenched.

Then, from out behind a rusted dumpster, a filthy old woman burst screaming at the shrouded man. He spun, as shocked as I was, and nearly jumped out of his own cheap loafers.

"You leave her alone!" the woman cried, wrapping her

skinny arms around the pursuer.

He swore at her, flailed, and struggled to break free from the rancid attack. The woman had a desperate air about her, like she had been wronged before. But the man had had enough of the bag of bones clinging to his body and he disappeared his glinting blade somewhere into its rags. The woman released and slowly slumped face-down to the ground.

As it played out, the sky grew lighter and early risers had begun to walk the sidewalk at the edge of the alley. There's no doubt they saw a shady man, a surprised woman, and a homeless person hunched on the ground, but none of them intervened. Typical normie behavior: never caring about anything perceived lesser than themselves. "None of my business," they undoubtedly thought. Thankfully, however, this morning their eyes alone were enough to send this cowardly man scrambling from the scene.

Every muscle in my body melted back to room temperature once the alley was clear. I released my hold on my knife and rushed over to the woman's side. I rolled her over and saw the stab wound at the edge of her waist. She was still awake, just in shock. Her eyes were kind and dark and her hair was a pleasant nest of deep black and light grey. Her skin was even blacker due to the filth, but underneath laid a beautiful shade of umber. At one time she may have been gorgeous.

"We need to get you to a hospital," I said stupidly before

thanking her.

"No," she replied. "No hospitals. I have nothing left."

"Jesus," I blurted, just as stupidly, then, "How did you end up like this?"

What? I'm not allowed to be curious about normies sometimes?

After some heavy breathing she began: "My husband passed from cancer. Three years ago. We had been swimming in medical bills all the way up to his death and beyond. It didn't matter how much money we made, how much we had saved, the hospital still found a way to drown me."

I should probably add that since Shifters can manipulate so much of their DNA, normie illnesses never seem to stick to us. Maybe that's our superpower. Either way, I felt for her. She had risked her miserable life to save a no-good Shifter and there I was giving her the third degree.

Suddenly an idea popped into my head. One that felt like an unsolicited knock on the doorway to my soul. A strange plan that didn't totally revolve around myself for once.

"Can you walk?" I asked.

She nodded and I helped her to her feet. With her arm hanging on my shoulder, and mine supporting her waist, we hobbled out of the alley and back to the billionaire's hotel underneath the light of the morning sun. We entered through a side door to avoid prying eyes and headed straight to the suite I fulfilled a sick fantasy inside mere hours ago. And it just *had* to be on the top floor.

After the grueling elevator ride I propped the woman up against the door while I dug in my purse for the keycard. I always swipe one in case of emergencies like this. Well, not exactly like this, but you get the picture. My fingers found the card hiding between the knife and the money—two cold reminders of my day thus far—and since checkout wasn't for another few hours it worked like a charm.

Inside I sat the woman on an overtly expensive leather chair near the entryway. Then I rushed over to a cart filled with silver trays of uneaten food and wheeled it back to her. "Eat as much as you want," I said. She grimaced right away, but seemed to lighten up at the thought of a full meal.

While she ate I grabbed the first aid kit stationed underneath the bathroom sink and patched the woman up as good as I could. And by "patch" I mean cleaned off the wound and slapped a wad of gauze on top. It looked to me like the knife missed anything crucial for staying alive and instead just cut a deep gash in her dark skin. Most importantly, there was food in her belly and tape on her wound, though her appearance remained filthy.

"You should take a hot shower," I encouraged.

The woman shakily downed a glass of water, then nodded. She lifted herself from the chair with strength she had not realized in years, despite the stab wound, then asked, "Why are you going through all of this trouble for me?"

I shrugged. We both knew neither of our kind did the other any favors. "Because you went through the trouble for me."

She accepted and went into the bathroom for a long overdue bathing. Once she shut the door, I leaned my back against it and sighed a heavy sigh. I could hear her stiff, sooted clothing hit the pristine tile floor. I could hear the nozzles squeak open. I could hear her cold skin absorb the warm water as the grime was swept away.

"Tell me about your husband," I said loud enough so she could hear.

This seemed to jump-start her long-withered optimism because words about her late lover's life came pouring from out the shower mist. His career as a carpenter, his persistent birdwatching, their favorite hiking trails, and on and on and on. I had to interrupt.

"What did he look like? Do you have a picture?"

The upbeat voice behind the door grew quiet, then said sadly, "All I have is a memory."

This put a damper on my brilliant plan so I thought for a few moments. "Could you describe him to me?"

The woman paused, then began in great detail. Effortlessly. It was as if she had never missed a single day with him. Like he lived on vibrantly as the only thing smiling inside her mind. My skin began to tingle.

Eventually the water stopped and the woman emerged from the steamy bathroom wrapped in a fresh cotton robe. Her skin now smooth as silk, her hair now thick and rejuvenated with volume, and she now looked half as old as

I thought she had been. Then the mist cleared and she laid eyes on me.

I don't know what I expected to happen next. Was she supposed to collapse? Scream? Run? I had never done anything like this before, let alone based on the description of a ghost from the past. I must have nailed it though because instead of freaking out her hand slowly covered her trembling lips. Her eyes each blinked a tear down her cheeks, and she said softly, "I've missed you so much."

After a few moments frozen in front of each other, I noticed a dark spot growing on the side of the robe that covered her wound and realized my previous assessment was wildly miscalculated. How much time we had left was now out of my hands.

I led her over to the plush, oversized bed meant for new lovers and sat down quietly. Saying something that I think her dead husband whom I have never met might say didn't feel quite right, so I decided to stay silent. This was her time, not mine.

Over the next few hours I discovered that some normies could still be human, even when everything had been taken from them. For a while we just lied next to each other, me on my back with her nestled beside like two puzzle pieces had found their only fit. My arm wrapped around her shoulder and hers hugged at my waist. She talked for a while. I listened. But mostly we absorbed each other. Nothing romantic. And I thought, was this a glint of what I had long desired?

Eventually the ins and outs of the woman's loving breaths ceased. The stain on her robe had grown significantly, but I'm convinced that's not what killed her. The memory she had of her husband was the only thing keeping her alive those last three years, and I had just given her the permission she needed to let them go. It was unintentional, but it felt right. Like I had used a lantern of love to light my darkness instead of continually tossing fuel on the ugly fire of fetish.

A knock on the door interrupted my train of thought, followed by, "Housekeeping!"

Right on time. I hopped up from the bed while simultaneously shifting out of a dead man's skin. I grabbed my purse, tipped over the cart of food, and scattered the woman's rags.

"Housekeeping!" I heard again.

"I'm coming!"

When I flung the door open the housekeeper's eyes widened, then looked away in shame. "Sorry, Mr. Greenburg. I had no idea you were still—"

"Get out of my way!" I barked with his voice, startling her further.

Quickly, I exited the room, making sure to look up at the hallway cameras and wink as I passed under. The doors of the elevator parted and I entered casually. *Lobby*, I selected, then smiled when a blood-curdling shriek came from down the hallway just before the doors had closed . . .

I guess what exited at the bottom was me. The *true* me.

The new me that's sitting on this bus writing a bunch of nonsense some normie might read someday yet never believe. I'm done with the Night Shift. I have to be. It hollowed me out. I've discovered that the only way to fill myself back up with happiness—*true* happiness—is by giving it to others who need it more. Going forward, fulfillment is my new price. And revenge on that billionaire who tried to whack me? Well, that was just a self-satisfying tip for going through all the trouble.

VALØUR

Private Williams stuck his cane into the mud, fell, then broke his hip. A battalion of soldiers sauntered over his sinking body as black gunfire cracked and hovered around them like cancerous clouds. Six inch shells shot from Howitzers shook the ground beneath. Corporal Connelly was soon felled to hands and knees in search of his fallen glasses, but they too were swallowed by the bloodsoaked earth.

Above, two Supermarine Spitfires spat high-caliber rounds from their throats at the targeted ridge. A long strip of blinding fire, curdled howls, and enemy bodies were sent hurtling through the air. The battalion cheered with invigorated love for queen and country as the planes continued their growl towards the horizon.

"Did you hear that?" Lance Corporal Hoult cried while lifting a fallen soldier to his feet.

The soldier held a bent horn up to his muddy ear and said, "Huh?"

"That sweet burbling music!" Hoult cried even louder, "That's the sound of victory!"

"Yes, these mounds are slippery!" the soldier confirmed, then hobbled onward.

Slowly, the two opposing sides converged until the smoke revealed each other's dirt-ridden faces. White eyes popped from their soiled expressions like flickering stars in a grim sky. They all dropped to the ground and leveled their guns with weary, wrinkled hands. A veil of thick smolder rolled through the gap, shrouding their scopes, and then...

Rrrrraaaaaeeeeerrrrr!

The siren sounded at four o'clock. Expectedly. Always.

At once all of the troops relinquished their positions and drifted back to their respective camps. Chairs and tables were set out across what remained of a grassy field, their legs held firmly in place by the drying mud. After a time Lance Corporal Hoult spotted Corporal Connelly bumbling around and guided him by the arm to an empty table. They both unslung the rifles from around their shoulders, leaned them against the chair backs, and fell into their seats.

"Lost your spectacles again, old chap?" Hoult asked of

his squinting comrade.

"Bloody hell," Connelly chuffed, shaking his head. He reached into a satchel hidden behind his lapel and retrieved a new pair, then balanced them on his nose. "Thank blazes it's tea time!"

"Aye. Now where is that nippy with our Earl Grey?"

Hoult looked behind to an elderly lady stepping out from the canvas field tent and eyed her from head to toe. She wore a brown side cap, a khaki button-down shirt with matching short pants, and brown boots that housed wool stockings stretched up to her knobby knees. In her hands she carried a small silver tray balancing a teapot and two cups. The woman stole a brief pause after each careful step; as if not to slip and waste any tea on the mud.

"Taking her sweet time, innit?" Connelly chuffed again.

"Oh, hush down," Hoult replied with a grin. "Gives us more opportunity to admire her strong legs."

"Speaking of . . . How are the wife and kids?"

Hoult returned his attention to the table, heavily leaned back in his chair, then sighed. "Martha's been struggling with stairs. Sent me a letter last week saying Johnny and Meg popped by to move our bed to the ground floor."

Connelly nodded with understanding. "Shame, that."

Just then, in the same way the falling sun lengthens a noon shadow, another soldier emerged stumbling from the blighted battlefield. A soldier unknown to them.

Hoult put a hand up to his brow. "Is that Private

Williams?"

"'Fraid not," Connelly said. Then, rising from his chair, he added, "Poor soul looks out of sorts."

Hoult remained at the table as Connelly shuffled over to aid the lost soldier. The original hue of the stranger's uniform had been washed away by weeks of rain and mud and bloodshed, but they were certain he was not amongst their ranks. When Connelly finally returned, he sat the disheveled man down on the remaining chair at the table across from Hoult.

"Grazie," the man said. His head held a constant jitter like a nerved metronome. "Thank you."

Hoult pulled a short pipe from his pocket, puffed some life into it, and leaned forward. "An Italian chap, eh? What brings you to this neck of the woods?"

All three of the men burst into sobering laughter that settled just as the elderly lady arrived with their tea. She set the tray delicately on the table and poured out two cups for the men on her side. She stared at the third.

Hoult, sensing her hesitance, said, "My good lady, could you retrieve a third cup for our annexed guest?"

"But sir," she said through a nervous grin, "He fights for the *other* side."

"Nonsense! We are all allies at tea time. I insist!"

With that, the elderly lady saluted, then started back towards the tent. One step. Pause. One step. Pause. One step...

"Now," Hoult continued, "What's your name and how do you come to find yourself amidst our platoon?"

The Italian man thought for quite a moment. "Luigi," he finally said with a thick accent. Then, "And I can't recall. It seems the loud gunfire has stolen my memory instead of my life."

"Should we all be so lucky," confided Connelly with a nod.

Two smoke rings rose above Hoult's head. "What *can* you remember, old chap?"

Luigi's head shook out a smile. "I remember my granddaughter, Stella. And my great-granddaughter Rosa, whom I have yet to meet." He reached into his pocket and retrieved a grainy photo of a young woman holding a newborn. Unlike Luigi, they both had thick heads of dark hair.

Hoult leaned over to have a look, then grunted in approval. "That's a fine family you've made," he said, "So much life to live. My granddaughter is to be wed in December to a good man. Connelly's is about to graduate Oxford."

Connelly nodded. "Top of his class at twenty-four. I'm glad such a mind isn't wasted on these bloody hills."

"A bunch of bollocks, really," Hoult tossed in with some heat. "The thought of children in these fields of battle. Don't you agree, Luigi?"

"Certo. Yes. I am thankful to be fighting for their chance to be better."

Hoult slapped the table with his palm, splashing brown tea over the brim of his cup. "Could not have said it better myself!"

The three were musing jovially on their kin, and their kin's kin, when the elderly lady finally returned with a third cup for Luigi. They grew quiet while she poured with shaky hands, and Hoult watched her with studious eyes as she leaned over. Then some more as she carefully crossed the mud to the field tent once again.

"Have you caught wind of the madness Parliament is proposing?" Connelly asked, goading Hoult's attention back to the table. When all ears were fixed on him he dipped his head and added, "Lowering the age of enlistment to fifty..."

Hoult nearly spat out his tea with a grumble. "What do those pillocks think this is? America?"

"Italia is considering the same," Luigi quavered. "Mussolini even suggested as low as twenty. Said they are robusto, tough, and can run faster."

Connelly chortled at the thought. "Run faster to what? Death? That manky git."

After a few puffs from his pipe, Hoult decided to speak vehemently. "Well I won't have it! The war to end all wars halts in eighteen, and what does the old world do? Starts a bigger one in thirty-nine! It's our fight, and I will not see the blood of our youngest and brightest spilled on these plains!"

"Here, here!" Connelly added, holding out his mug. Hoult's raised to join it, and Luigi's followed shakily. All three cups clanked, then they downed their unifying tea with valour.

The lively conversation had pushed time to the backs of the soldiers' minds and they were staggered when the elderly woman returned with her serving tray. She placed the three cups—Luigi's last—top down on the silver surface, and wished Hoult and Connelly a good day. As her mosey marshaled her back across the mud, a familiar sound filled the air.

Rrrrraaaaaeeeeerrrrr!

"Well old chaps, duty calls!" said Hoult as he stole one last puff before tucking his pipe away.

Both the Lance Corporal and Corporal rose to their feet and lifted the rifles leaning against their chairs. Luigi, using the sturdy table to assist his trembling body upright, was shot dead to the ground before he could even say goodbye.

This was war, after all.

¡FANTASMA!

Not far into the hills southwest of Guadalajara, if you know where to look, stands the oldest and most treasured hotel in all of Mexico. It is not renowned for its size, nor its clientele, but for the unique experience it provides to the most curious of travelers. In fact, if you were cruising the dusty backroads of the southern altiplano, you would not be remiss for passing by the three-room inn nestled snugly behind an arched wall unnoticed. Yet there it always has been. Resting amongst the shady overgrowth, with an open vacancy to all those daring enough to darken its doorstep, lies the Casa Fantasma.

It was this same arched entry that Mr. Crosby's cactus-green Cadillac convertible overtook a good three or four times before turning into. The archway was bordered by a long adobe wall that had been cracked by time and sun, and seemed only to be held together by stringy, button-leafed vines. Leading up to the inn, the deep black tires of the brand-new Cadillac crunched along a lengthy driveway of spotless white gravel until reaching a large covered pergola that dripped orange-flowered tendrils over its eaves. Mr. Crosby parked under the overhang and took satisfaction in that his was the only vehicle present. One could never be too careful of door dings.

After stretching his stiffened legs, smoothing out the travel-worn wrinkles from his tailored ivory suit, and adjusting the brim of his matching fedora, he retrieved a sizable leather briefcase from the trunk of his car and started towards the inn, but not before running a cloth over the fingerprints he had left on the cactus-green paint.

The Casa Fantasma was a peculiar building in Mr. Crosby's eyes, but nothing extraordinary. It was a single floor adobe structure with peach-colored bricks running across the corners and roof like an emboldened tracing. A perfectly manicured garden of evergreen succulents, vibrant flowers, and swaying palms made up the surrounding grounds, and spiky blue agaves poked up from the earth to line the walkway leading up to the front door—a masterclass in arid landscaping. Curious to Mr. Crosby, however, was the absence of sprinklers, fountains, or hose-bearing employees, and that the inn somehow flourished in spite of Mexico's ongoing drought.

At the arched, windowless door, Mr. Crosby lifted his right hand to rap on the greying wood when a brick suddenly fell from the roof and cracked in half near his left foot. He did not even shift his weight. "You'll have to be more clever than that," he smirked, then knocked three times.

Immediately the door swung open to reveal an old man with a wide mustache and an even wider smile. His wrinkles creased deep with his words. "Hola amigo! Welcome to Casa Fantasma!"

"Greetings, Diego. I trust everything is in order for my visit?"

"Si, Señor Crosby," Diego nodded with pride. "You will not be disappointed on this night."

"Three nights, actually," Mr. Crosby replied with a nod of his own. "That is the required amount of time to conduct a full report."

"Lo siento, of course! Come in, come in. Allow me to show you around this enchanting hotel!"

The inn was small. Mr. Crosby was first met with less of a reception area and more of an extended entryway that spread outwards. To the left was a blank wall with hooks for coats, and to the right was a small dining area to which they entered. To the left again, a short mahogany bar accompanied by two stools was the focal point of pride. Hanging above the counter was a multilayered lattice housing deep red bottles of wine that absorbed the sun from a skylight above. Behind was a large mirror framed by mahogany shelving built specifically to display awards earned from past publications. Mr. Crosby squinted to read their captions, then rolled his eyes at each falsity. Three circular dining tables occupied the rest of the room and a window faced outward to the immaculate garden. As explained by Diego, everything was hand-crafted centuries ago.

Traveling through and around the public area was another archway that led to the remainder of the inn. Appearing longer than the hotel itself was a narrow, skylit hallway housing six closed doors. An intricately patterned runner stretched across the rich floorboards. Behind two of the doors, Diego charmingly briefed, was storage and the kitchen, one held his personal quarters, and the remaining three were reserved for visitors. "Per your request, Señor Crosby, you will be our only guest during your visit."

"*Our?*" Mr. Crosby repeated. He had not witnessed anyone in the garden or dining area. "Are there other employees I should be aware of?"

"No, lo siento! Just a figure of speech. You will encounter only myself at Casa Fantasma."

Mr. Crosby scanned the dark corners of the hallway with skepticism. "I'll be the judge of that."

Diego looked up at his visitor puzzled. "Did you not come all this way as a believer, Señor Crosby?"

"I believe, Diego, that there is a difference between being

haunted, and being hoodwinked."

The steps that followed were in silence until they reached the last door on the left. Diego removed a golden ring of seven skeleton keys from his belt and inserted one into the lock until a sharp *click!* returned.

The room behind the door was quaint, filled with opulent, hand-crafted fixtures that no doubt shared the same origins as those from the dining room. At the far end was a large, decorative bed with four thick posts rising from the corners to prop up a canopy. An ornate nightstand stood next to it. Opposite the bed was a wide dresser with a matching mirror above. And to the immediate left was a beautiful desk and chair that could have each been carved from the same exact tree. Not a speck of dust could be seen. If Mr. Crosby had been there for quality alone, he would be nearly impressed.

"The breakfast is at eight de la mañana," Diego said, interrupting the silence that had grown rather quickly, "and the bar is always open!" Then Diego turned, but before starting back down the hallway he poked his head back through the door. "Oh, and Señor Crosby? I suspect by the end of your visit, you will know the difference."

When Diego disappeared, Mr. Crosby locked the door from the inside and laid his leather briefcase on the warm wood of the desk. He pinched two silver latches until they popped open, raised the lid. Inside were three outfits, a thick robe, books on physics and atmospheric phenomena, his

Moleskine journal, and two fountain pens. He sat down on the desk's matching chair, then opened his journal to begin writing when a stack of old clippings praising his work slid out from the inside cover. *"Haunted" Hotel Crumbles to Columnist Crosby*, he recalled fondly. *Journalist Jinxes Bewitched B&B. Ghostly Guesthouse A Gaff, Crosby Confirms.* One by one he laid the articles out, smiling wider with each passing headline.

That night Mr. Crosby found it easy to pass into slumber. His eyes were heavy from his days of travel and the large canopied bed was exceptionally comfortable. However, late into the night, somewhere between the darkest and dawn, he was stirred by a sharp *click!* coming from the door's direction. His eyes shot open eagerly, alert. He was ready to begin his work.

Mr. Crosby sat up and watched the door handle jiggle. The latch had ticked free despite him specifically locking it after entering earlier that afternoon. He slipped out from underneath the covers and rushed over to the door just as it groaned open, seemingly on its own accord, then snatched the handle in his own hand and flung his head into the hallway. Empty. Wait! Invisible footsteps lightly thumped along the lengthy rug until flipping the end corner into the air before vanishing. Mr. Crosby only narrowed his eyes and returned to bed.

Around eight the next morning, Mr. Crosby sat sipping a complimentary cup of hot coffee at one of the three tables in the dining area. Steam rolled from the mug as he listened to Diego rambling on and on inside the kitchen across the hall. Mr. Crosby began to think it odd that the lonely innkeeper had so much to say to himself when he burst from the door carrying a hot plate of tortillas, beans, eggs, tomato, and avocado.

"Huevos rancheros for our special guest!" Diego said, crinkling his face with a proud smile.

"There's that word again," Mr. Crosby pointed out, "*Our*. You are certain it is only you that operates this establishment? No artful assistant? No cunning custodian?"

"Apologies, Señor Crosby. Old habits." Diego winked, then added, "How did you sleep?"

"Exceptionally well," Mr. Crosby said, nearly surprising himself with the compliment, "though I was stirred before dawn."

"Stirred, señor?"

"Yes. It seemed that my locked door suddenly became unlocked and it creaked itself open; yet I do not remember it creaking when I entered. A trick mechanism, to be sure. Then there were audible footsteps leading away from my room, but they are explained away as simply as the lock: You've hired someone to stand beneath the floorboards with boots on their hands. The technique is a tired staple among haunters, really."

"Is it now?" Diego asked with a slight nod; the kind that feigned polite interest in a one-sided conversation.

"I will admit," Mr. Crosby continued before the innkeeper could exit, "that the subtle flip of the carpet at the end was a nice touch. How did you accomplish that?"

Diego's smile returned alongside a shrug. "How should I know, Señor Crosby? I was asleep."

The second night, just before dawn, Mr. Crosby awoke to a strange chill nipping at his bones. His groggy eyes opened to a condensed cloud of breath escaping his mouth. He was shivering.

His arm stretched for his glasses on the accompanying nightstand and noticed something even more peculiar; there was no frost on the lenses. In fact, his hand felt warmth as it escaped the border of his bed frame. Once he rested the spectacles on his nose he looked over to the dresser and, more importantly, the mirror above. No frost clung to its surface either!

Mr. Crosby leapt from the ice-cold sheets and dropped down to the floor on his hands and knees. The sudden jolt pained his frozen joints. He shook off the discomfort then peered under the large frame. No cooling pipes could be seen in the pale morning light, nor was any machinery at play. Unable now to rest in that bitter bed, Mr. Crosby slung on his robe and left for the dining area in a huff.

Diego arrived laughing with the rising sun to witness Mr. Crosby combing through a well-worn book on thermodynamics. His guest donned a thick robe and was gulping hot coffee as if it were ice water at midday.

"You're up early, Señor Crosby!" Diego chided as he crossed the bar on his way to the kitchen. "I trust you slept well?"

"Clever trick, Diego," Mr. Crosby said, bypassing any pleasantries. He slapped his book on the table and pointed to a lengthy paragraph on an open page. "Heat transfer. I've seen it before, but never executed this seamlessly. While I could not locate them, my hypothesis is that there are pipes built directly into the frame of my bed, carrying a coolant of some sort to a condenser nearby. What eludes me, though, is that I could not hear any machinery running. Where have you hidden it?"

"Señor?" Diego asked, as if he understood only half the words in Mr. Crosby's sudden lecture.

"Your air conditioner. Is it outside? No, I would have seen it by now. Perhaps in the hallway closet? Show me."

Lowering his raised eyebrows, the innkeeper simply smiled and retrieved his golden keyring. "Follow me, vámonos."

They went to the hallway closet across from the kitchen and Diego unlocked it. All that was inside was freshly jarred spices, sundries, snacks, and supplies for serving them on. Nothing more.

On the third and final night, Mr. Crosby was roused at a time unknown to him. He would admit that, for the first time in decades, he had had some trouble falling asleep, but was well under it before being stirred. It started with an incessant ticking, like the kind one would hear from the reel of a moving picture, that eventually lit up the room with a ghostly aura.

Mr. Crosby sat up. There was light, but no visible source. He retrieved his glasses, fumbled them over his ears, then leaned forward until the mirror above the dresser was in clear view. Inside, yes inside, the mirror was a colorless playback from Mr. Crosby's youth. He had just been shoved to the ground and was inspecting the black blood beading in his palms. It was Halloween. Above him stood three older boys, no, ghosts, draped in shapeless white sheets that had dark, soulless holes cut into the places where eyes should have been. With unseen hands they were filling their plastic pumpkins with the candy that had spilled out from his own. Laughter and ridicule ensued. His heart began to ache.

Suddenly, water droplets started falling all around Mr. Crosby. Like wet fingers they tapped on every surface except for himself. "No!" he cried, concerned for his case and clippings, then launched towards the desk. Not a single drop of water touched him along the way. When he reached them, his belongings, too, were dry as the arid air.

Deciding enough was enough, Mr. Crosby hastily dressed, packed up his belongings, and stormed out of the last room on the left. He was completely dry except for the soles of his shoes.

At the other end of the long hallway he abruptly turned the corner to find Diego sitting jovially on one of the stools at the bar. A single light shone down through the hanging lattice above onto two half-filled glasses of deep red wine.

"Señor Crosby!" Diego said with glee, "Come to join us for a drink?

Too flushed to notice the phrasing, or the second wine glass, Mr. Crosby commanded, "Where did you get that projection?"

"Señor?"

"Have you been following me all of these years? Another disgruntled peddler of ghost stories, just waiting for the right moment to humiliate me?"

"Claro que no," Diego eased. "I have been right here my whole life."

Mr. Crosby paced back and forth in short bursts. "Then you use sprinklers hidden in the ceiling to dump water all over my life's work? That's no way to treat a guest, Diego. You and your hidden assistant should be ashamed!"

Bewildered, Diego leaned over to inspect Mr. Crosby's suit and briefcase under the low light. He was dry as the Mexican sand. "Señor, if I have done anything to disrupt your stay—"

"Enough," Mr. Crosby said with ice in his voice. He turned and jammed a finger towards the elderly innkeeper. "My article on this establishment will *not* be kind. All of your distasteful tricks will be exposed and no one will *ever* spend a peso at Casa Fantasma again!"

With that, Mr. Crosby clutched his briefcase tightly and

fled to the door, slamming it heavily on his way out. But before he made it to the pergola covering his Cadillac, he overheard chatter protruding from the open window of the dining area, and halted. *I knew there was someone else!*

Mr. Crosby crept back quietly and peered through the opening, careful not to be seen.

Diego still sat at the bar but his glass of red wine was raised out in front of him. "Well, mi amigo," he said brightly, "we had a good run, no? Salud!"

Then, unexpectedly, the second glass of red wine floated up from the counter and clinked against Diego's in solidarity. *Wires, clearly,* thought Mr. Crosby, but the aerial display had not yet completed. The hovering glass tipped its stem upwards and the red wine disappeared into thin air.

JOBS
FOR ALL
JOBS
FOR ALL

THE LINE

By 8:15 in the morning the line had already reached the bottom of the cliffside trail. Sunlight climbed slowly over the ridge, which seemed to keep pace with the steadily shuffling footsteps. The craggy sidewalls, grated against by decades of erosive wind and punishing sunlight, lost fragments to the wind with each and every gust, leaving behind hollow cracks in the rock. Howard thumbed away a thin layer of new dust from his equally-cracked watch and was delighted he had arrived before five a.m. *The early bird gets the worm,* he thought, even though everyone was guaranteed a worm today.

Though the line had already filled itself in the previous night, Howard was pleased to discover the efficiency at which it kept advancing. By his estimate, thousands stood before him and thousands more stood behind, though counting their exact numbers was restricted by a wooden fence lining the narrow path that zigged and zagged its way up to the summit. Because of this barrier he could not predict if his wait would last several more hours or several more days. Either way, as long as the line kept moving, he would not be one to complain.

To pass the time Howard liked to imagine what the world was like before. He was still an infant when the sky was blue, so memories were scarce, and his mind often failed to picture his surroundings in the vivid colors of the past. When he looked to his left he could only see the unattractive combination of tan sandstone and grey limestone that made up the cliff walls. When he looked to his right there was the tall, colorless fence hastily constructed with splintered planks that denied any glimpse of the other side. The barrier was assumedly there to keep people from falling over the ridge, but Howard could not help but wonder if it was also sparing him a depressing view of the dried riverbed below.

When he grew dismal from thinking about the same two shades of the same two colors he had absorbed his entire life, Howard shifted his attention to the posters hanging on the makeshift wall.

"Guaranteed job placement for everyone," he read aloud

to himself. "Walk-in interviews begin at eight a.m. starting November 15th."

Howard cringed at the image depicting a sanguine worker wearing a hard hat because he had once been an accountant and hoped he would not have to do anything back-breaking. Of course it was only a familiarized image representing the working class, but callused hands would simply be a waste of his mathematical talent. After all, he believed, the best positions should go to those who had gotten in line as early as he.

"A guaranteed job for everyone? Ha! What a load of government shit!" the man directly behind Howard blurted. "They're the reason there ain't no jobs to begin with!"

Howard reactively turned only to capture a quick glance at the boisterous man, but his movement was too noticeable. They had already made eye contact.

"You agree, don't ya?" the man goaded with a throat full of gravel. "We all had jobs, food, and a warm place to sleep before those spineless bureaucrats started lettin' everyone reproduce again."

Howard felt cornered, but was tragically too polite to ignore him. He knew that the Population Bill had gone sour, but he also knew it would be futile attempting to sway a stranger's certitude. Plus confrontation made Howard squirm, so he only replied with, "Again?"

"Right! They don't acknowledge it, but we know the damn truth. It all started when... Oh, I'm sorry, guy. How rude of me. Name's Dean Richards."

Dean held his hand out for Howard to shake and Howard hesitated for an awkward second. This action would seal his commitment to the conversation. Ultimately, he was just too polite not to return the gesture.

"And this is my daughter... Hey, where is she?"

Dean and Howard both swiveled, careful not to lose their positions in line, and immediately spotted a young girl trying to scale the tall fence. She had very light hair, almost white under the blanched sun, and a small ragdoll hung from her back pocket.

"Natalie, get down from there!" Dean barked, more miffed than worried.

Natalie's foot slipped as soon as her dad's voice reached her. She daintily recovered, hopped down from the top of the fence, landed clumsily, then skipped back over to her father. She clenched onto Dean's legs and glanced at Howard between them.

Dean looked down and said, "I told you, Nat, you have to stay next to me while we're waitin' in line."

"Daddy, that building is ginorm—"

"Not now, sweetie," Dean dismissed, patting the young girl's head. "Can't you see that me and... Hey, what's your name anyway?"

"M-my name?" Howard stuttered, knowing he was now glued to this conversation permanently. "It's H-Howard. Howard B-Buchanan."

"Okay Nat, me and Howard are talking now. You can play around, but stay off of that damn wall. Your mother would kill me if you fell off the edge."

"Fine," Natalie sighed. She looked back at Howard and then went to play with her doll by some crumbling rocks.

"Now, where were we? Oh yeah…"

Howard was just noticing that both the doll and the little girl had very light hair when a foreign memory came rushing by him like an impetuous breeze. For a moment he was suspended in air, looking up at a woman with golden hair and a bright cerulean shirt. Smiling with radiant red lips, she slowly set him down and his head fell to the side. He could now see outside through an open window. There was an ocean of green grass underneath an endless span of blue sky. This was a place where everything felt natural, yet so far out of reach. As he rotated his head back to see the comforting woman once more, her face was replaced with Dean Richard's.

" … and that's why every damned thing is brown now," Dean trailed, immediately aware of the lack of response he felt he deserved. "Howard? Howard? You still in there, bub?"

Howard shook his head. "Yes, sorry. My mind just wandered for a second."

"I know what ya mean. I start seein' red when I so much as think about people fornicatin' without proper documentation. But everyone thinks they're so damn special; that they can just keep poppin' out kids left and right and there will magically be enough food and work to go 'round. Bah! I got my license to have one child and you just met her."

"I'm not sure that's—"

"Sorry, I couldn't help but overhear," interrupted the woman standing in front of Howard in line—thankfully. "But the government can't just abolish a basic human right. It's *our* decision if we want to bear children or not! Always had been, always should be."

Dean immediately loaded a rebuttal in his chamber and pulled the trigger. "Listen, lady—"

"Julie."

"Listen, Julie, that's exactly the kind of thinkin' that got us standin' in line on top of a damn cliff just to get some underpaid, state-issued vocation. Because of overpopulation, every job worth takin' is took, every drink of water is drank, and every inch of growable ground has grown its last!"

"Oh, and you think the Population Bill was a justified measure from our fearless leaders? To force families to register for a child and then get Big Brothered from conception to birth? The riots alone nearly started a war!"

"Those riots only started because a bunch of damn Bible-thumpers were losing subscribers. They should've never revoked that bill. I had my kid fair 'n' legal and couldn't be happier. What's a little paperwork anyway if you can walk down the street without stepping over a homeless body every few feet?"

Howard shifted his stance because his ears and feet were

beginning to hurt. He knew those two would continue their argument for a while, so he did not mind tuning out. He checked his cracked watch again, realized it was after lunch, and started to get hungry. After fantasizing about Aliment for a good while, he looked up and noticed the front of the line had just come into view, and there was a colossal building silhouetted behind them. He must have shuffled miles uphill that morning and had not even realized it.

While the squabble persisted, and so did his hunger, Howard started to wonder about this peculiar location the government chose to build its new plant. The construction of the gigantic ziggurat had been covered on the news for months; presumably to create awareness for all of the incredible new employment opportunities. It had a unique, pyramid-esque design that almost resembled an ancient Mesopotamian temple. While not exactly a triangle, each layer, or step, had a definite slope towards the top. Perhaps each promotion moved an employee up a floor into the smaller, more exclusive sections. Howard then remembered the commercials advertising the construct as, "A modern-day Babel sure to attract the masses."

But why at the top of this cliff? Was it the only available land that Sahara Industries had not already owned? Was it because the flat, barren summit could support a new structure built to accommodate tens of thousands of people? Or was this clifftop wasteland the most sardonically appropriate place to put a pyramid? Either way, Howard relished the idea that he might obtain an office overlooking the others waiting in line. *That* would make the entire day spent on his feet well worth the effort.

"Look on the bright side, at least they're trying something," Howard bravely interrupted out of nowhere, stopping both Dean and Julie from their discourse. "You know, putting up this building to give all of these people a purpose again."

Howard could see the gears in their heads begin to rotate after long being jammed with rusted thoughts. He did not appreciate that both of them were turning this pragmatic and positive gathering into a political argument. These days everyone was broke, hungry, and sometimes homeless, but there was always hope.

"You're right," Julie finally conceded with a heavy sigh. "We should try to see a little more color in this grey situation."

Dean had calmed, but was still skeptical. "Eh, I don't know. Something about standin' in line all day just rubs me the wrong way. But hey, I've got Nat and the missus to feed."

Howard dug into his newfound traction. "Well I for one am excited. Any one of us could get a nice office at the top of this brand new building and live comfortably for the rest of our lives. There might be an option to travel, perhaps they provide benefits, and hey, maybe we'll even get to play a role in reforestation!"

Even Dean could not stop his mouth from grinning. All three of them got to chatting after Howard's intervention and forgot what they were mad about in the first place. Howard learned that Julie had managed the produce department at a grocery store and, despite her opinions, had three legal children under the Population Bill, while Dean once owned his own gas station up until the fossil fuel industry ran dry. Howard could not relate with a family of his own, but they all vaguely remembered when there was color. The positive conversation led them to lose track of time and they had not realized that the front of the line approached.

"Jesus, Mary, and Joseph, that building is ginormous!" Dean blurted.

"They weren't kidding when they said there would be room for everyone," Julie exhaled in awe. "I wonder how many stories that is?"

"Next!" a uniformed official cried out.

They all looked at each other.

"Guess this is my stop," Julie remarked, but before she reached the information table she made sure to turn and smile at Howard and Dean. "I suppose I'll see you in there!"

The remaining two made small talk until Julie followed another official inside the building.

"Next!"

This one was for Howard.

"Good luck, bub," Dean encouraged.

Howard nodded. As he walked up to the table he remembered to button up his sport coat and straighten his tie. He then brushed off a small pile of dust from his shoulders and watched it wisp into the air. It had been a long day of standing in line and he hoped he did not smell too bad.

"Name?"

"Uh, Howard. Howard Buchanan."

"Let's see . . . " The official looked through her list. "Ah, here you are. Accountant?"

"That's me! I was a CPA for 20 yea—"

"Right this way, follow me," insisted another official.

Howard saw the lady at the desk cross out his name and yell, "Next!" again. He was thrown by the impetuosity of the situation, but assured himself that this was only a formality to keep things moving and that the actual interview would take place inside.

As they approached the building Howard's neck strained from looking up. The unusual shape made it impossible to see the top. The official held the main door open for Howard and they both entered. They were greeted by solid walls and a dimly lit hallway that extended somewhere into the complex. Without a word, the official started down the passage and Howard followed.

"So are you the one I'm interviewing with? As you may have overheard, I was a CPA for over 20 years and I'm excited about this opportunity. I really think I'd be a valua—"

"Please step into the elevator," the official interrupted when they had reached the only gap in the seemingly endless tunnel.

"Oh, okay."

Howard stepped in. The center-opening doors immediately slammed behind him with a *clank!* and the elevator rapidly ascended up the shaft. Even at the accelerated speed the trip lasted for several minutes. When he finally felt the floor slow to a halt, the elevator doors released him to a vast, empty room. All was dark save for a few penetrating sunbeams from a skylight high above. The area gave the building an appearance of being hollow. He stepped further out into the emptiness in search of an office or employee or another hallway, but there was nothing.

Howard froze in place. His mind was racing with questions. Maybe this particular floor was still under construction. It was entirely plausible that they would hire others from the line to put the finishing touches on the interior. With that securely in mind, Howard quickly resolved that this was a simple misunderstanding and that he must have just gotten off on the wrong floor. However, when he started back for the elevator, the doors slammed shut and it immediately descended.

"This can't be right," Howard uttered under his breath. Then he shouted, "Hello!"

But as the final "o" left his mouth, he heard a *clunk!* followed by a mechanical whirring, almost like an amplified thrum. Then the floor began to shift, vibrating very slowly at first. Howard thought he had only lost his balance when the platform below started picking up speed. Fumbling, he tried to stand, but everything below him kept retracting, disappeared.

He fell.

Silently.

Alone.

Howard must have plummeted hundreds of feet before landing on a lumpy mass where both his legs and spine immediately shattered. From the acute and instant pain he blacked out for a time, then slowly regained consciousness, unable to move or speak. He wanted to cry for help, but all he could do was turn his head far enough to see the dim outlines of bodies—thousands of them—all crushed and contorted with warm life seeping from dreadful wounds.

The sight of the dark blood recalled the memory of his mother's lips. Back when the grass was green. When the sky was blue. When everything felt right in the world. Howard clenched his eyes tightly and a single tear ran down his numbed cheek. As he agonizingly adjusted his broken neck to look upwards, the vivid memory fleeted as quickly as it had come. All that remained was a dark interruption in the dim skylight above, and the crushing blow of Dean's body landing on top of him.

Å COMMITTEE OF CURIOUS COLLECTORS

Over some knolls, through some thickets, and at the center of an emerald glade, there stands a great elm tree. Great not only for its unrivaled size, but because it had somehow grown hollowly around the stump of an ancestor that fell many centuries ago. We know this because a fissure in the vast trunk has allowed scholars to enter and take many measurements and samples of the wood within.

Not far from the Great Elm, as it is now marketed, and extremely far from everything else, a small village has claimed the attraction as their own and tourists from all over the world sojourn there to admire the tree from the hours of nine in the morning to four in the afternoon. On a typical day they enter the Great Elm's hollow, they place their hands and set their bottoms upon the ancient stump, they take photographs of themselves seated with bright flashes, and they call their friends and relatives to tell them that they are there and the other is not. Then they go back to the village to eat meals and drink drinks and make noise and then they go to sleep.

But tourism is likely the least interesting topic of this tale. And in some ways, so is the Great Elm. What is particularly beguiling is what takes place in and around this setting while none are paying attention. You see, each month when the moon is at its fullest, a night not that unlike tonight, a committee of curious collectors gathers within that great elm tree to show and tell and discuss matters of great importance to them.

"Alright," said the brown bear as he placed a pair of human spectacles too small for his broad snout in front of a pair of dark and astute eyes. He then palmed to the fifteenth page of a gnarled notepad and touched a gnawed pencil to its paper using claws with far more dexterity than one might think. "Roll call."

"This is, like, the third time it's been the fifth we've done this," croaked the frog, something foreign rattling around inside her mouth. "You know we're all here."

The crow, who had just flapped in clutching a white plastic shopping bag between his claws, quickly hung it on an offshoot to get a jump on mocking the frog. "Oh, the third time of the fifth time! And what easy-to-remember number could that equal?"

As a reaction, the frog tilted her head, squinted one swampy eye, held up a glossy hand, and attempted arithmetic in the air with the help of her padded fingers.

"It's alright, little Froggy," cooed the nearby cow with comfort. She mostly fit inside the hollow and would never complain if she did not. "I struggle with anything over four, which is coincidentally the number of hooves and stomachs I have."

The crow rattled its syrinx to mimic a human's laugh, which spooked the raccoon, who had already looked sick to its stomach, then said, "I believe fifteen is the number you're counting towards."

"Enough!" growled the bear. "We've only just arrived and are already getting off track. It is my duty as founder of this committee to create and maintain our records." He waited for all inside the Great Elm to aim their attention towards him, then proceeded with attendance. "Frog?"

"Here!"

"Raccoon?"

A pair of beady eyes lost inside a black mask stared blankly from the shadows. Directly below them a guttural belch breached the air and assaulted the tuned noses of the rest. Most groaned, the bear sighed.

"Raccoon is here. Cow?"

"Here! And I might add that your new eyewear is quite distinguishing."

"Thank you, Cow. I found them lying right next to the object I'll be presenting tonight. Crow?"

"Here," came a child's voice—human, female, and roughly between the ages of five and nine.

The raccoon jumped again and mewled.

"Will you stop frightening the committee with your mimicry, Crow?"

"Sorry," apologized the massive black bird in the traditional forest tongue. "All in good fun."

"Indeed," the bear said, crossing off the squiggly line that he interpreted to be crow's name, then placed both the pencil and the notepad safely inside a nearby knothole.

Before the committee sat the broad trunk of the Great Elm's progenitor. Nine-hundred-ninety-nine rings in all, smooth and oiled by decades of human touch. Directly above, fireflies hovered brightly out of both kindness and the desire to be included in something greater than themselves.

"Next order of business," the bear officiated, "we will commence presentations. This moon's collection: objects required for human survival."

"Can I go first?" the crow asked, crinkling his plastic sack with a black claw.

The bear shook his brown head. "You went first last moon, so this moon you are last."

"Maybe I should go first," the raccoon stressed, standing

up on his hind legs and rubbing his bloated grey belly feverishly.

"Raccoon, we are trying to develop a fair and equal tradition. Cow is first this moon, then Frog, you, myself, and finally, Crow."

The raccoon dropped back down to all fours and tried to focus on the smoothened stump instead of his turbulent tummy.

"Best for last, then," added the crow.

"We'll see about that," tested the bear. He waited for silence yet again before nodding respectfully at the cow. "You may begin."

Hiding just behind her front right leg was an object the cow lifted with her mouth and placed on top of the old stump. The fireflies dropped about a foot lower in unison and burned slightly brighter. Sitting there was a near-empty plastic container that was once filled with liquid gold.

"I heard the farmer call it oil," said the cow.

For better views around the stump the frog hopped onto a petrified root and the raccoon inched to the edge, resting his paws and snout on the lip. The bear leaned and looked over the top of his new glasses as he found they added nothing to his eyesight. The crow's vision was superior to the others' and he could see just fine from a knotted growth he chose to perch on.

"Go on," said the bear.

"Well," the cow continued, "the farmer always complains

about his metal machines leaking this stuff when he's out in the fields and says he must always keep a bottle on him. Says we'd all be sunk without it."

The bear lifted the container and tried to make sense of the print on the label. "Fascinating. Crow, can you decipher these human markings?"

"All I can really read is five-double-u-thirty," translated the crow in forest tongue, "but I'm not sure what it could mean."

The frog had a query next. "You said this oil leaks into the ground," she started, something still rattling inside her mouth, "What happens then?"

"I'm not sure. All I know is that it's thick and it's black and it smells like death."

At this the troubled raccoon gulped audibly. The frog shivered. The fireflies blinked and separated for a moment, then grouped back. The crow nodded gravely as he had seen much from the sky.

"I'm sorry to use such vulgar language," added the cow, "but it's the truth."

The bear thought it best to move forward with the presentations so he removed the bottle of oil, set it inside the same knothole as the notepad and pencil, then said, "Thank you, Cow. The humans must be extremely reliant on this oil if they continue to use it so carelessly. Frog, would you like to go next?"

A sharp ribbit came that meant, "Yes!" and the frog

hopped up onto the stump's top and uncurled her long tongue for all to see. Stuck to it were metal coins of various sizes and colors.

"Oh my!" said the cow.

The crow's feathers around his neck fluffed up as the line of coins reflected in his eye.

After shaking the coins free from her tongue, the frog coiled it back into her mouth and spoke more clearly. "These get dropped on the ground all the time, I've noticed, and humans always look visibly upset when they've misplaced them."

The bear pinched one coin between two claws and held it up close to the fireflies' warm glow. There was a human face printed on one side. "Are these images of family members? Perhaps carried out of sentiment?"

"Could be," the frog agreed simply.

A polite squawk from the crow interjected their lack of guile. "Humans call it money. They give these monies to other humans in exchange for other things. I have loads back at the nest."

"Mmmoooney," the cow playfully sounded out.

"And what sort of thing would one of these monies obtain?" asked the bear.

The crow cackled. "From you? Likely a snout full of sprayed peppers!"

The bear gave the crow a quick and stern look. The crow squelched his laughter.

"From another human, I think one of these monies could get them one of those metal machines Cow was talking about."

"Wow!" exclaimed the frog. "Then these must be of incredible value!"

A crass moan came suddenly from within the hollow. The raccoon was still in a fit. "Alright, alright! Can I please present now?"

Noticing the raccoon's odd behavior this entire moon, the bear obliged and removed the coins from the table to store inside the knothole. As his back was turned, the raccoon leapt onto the ancient stump, hunched its fat body into a mound, then began hacking profusely. The rest of the committee's chatter fell unto gasps and the fireflies' movements became sporadic. Heaving and heaving the raccoon's movements went until out from its mouth slid a dark, char-grilled mass.

All of the members' jaws fell to the floor and the cow's knees became unsteady. The raccoon, however, jumped down from the stump he had just defiled feeling as fresh as morning dew.

"For Oak's sake, Raccoon," the bear boomed. "Cow is standing right there!"

The raccoon gave one more relieved shake from his release and said, "Well, how else was I supposed to bring it here?"

The crow snickered at the delightful macabre of the situation, but the cow still wavered. Eventually the frog retrieved her jaw from the floor and she asked, "But *why* did you bring it here?"

"It's a steak," the raccoon said proudly. Then, "Apologies to Cow, but the village waste bins are filled with the things. Always half-eaten or less."

The bear comforted the cow for a short while until she said all was well. He then spoke to the raccoon directly. "Half-eaten would imply that they are not that valuable to humans."

"That's the thing!" the raccoon countered. "They never seem to finish them, but they always seem to be eating them. Surely they wouldn't create so much waste if they didn't require these steaks to survive, right?"

"Wasteful indeed. Any insight, Crow?" asked the bear.

The crow was quiet. He had seen from above what happens at those types of farms, all the mud and congestion and sadness, but the cow was too close a friend to repeat such things in her company. "Not any that I can think of at the moment."

The bear nodded knowingly. "Very well. Raccoon, remove this obstruction from the Great Elm at once."

The raccoon climbed back up the stump and clenched the steak between his teeth once again, but not before saying, "Sorry, Cow," then ran outside to leave it with the night. When he returned, the cow told him that it was alright and that she was thankful for the knowledge it brough.

"Well then!" announced the bear excitedly. "I guess that

brings it to me."

All except one shifted closer to the stump for they knew that the bear frequently brought impressive items. *Not as impressive as mine*, thought the crow, though.

The bear reached into a separate darkened knothole and retrieved with both hands a transparent item and placed it gently upright at the center of the old stump. A container of sorts. Inside at the bottom was some white residue and to the top stood a green stick that poked out like some clear creature's protracted spine. The committee all recognized the object, but did not know why.

The bear then turned the container until a small caricature of himself faced them. "Look!" he exclaimed.

The frog, the cow, and the raccoon did so curiously. The crow smirked as much as his beak would allow.

"Every human I've ever encountered has been carrying one of these," the bear continued. "I've even tasted one of the delicious treats that sometimes fills it."

"I've seen these, too," said the frog.

"Me as well," added the cow. "The farmer's partner will sometimes bring her one."

The Raccoon had seen them too. "Yes! So many in the trash next to the steaks!"

The cow quavered once again at the raccoon's vocabulary.

"Exactly!" confirmed the bear. "Whatever this container holds, it is of dire need to the humans, and can only be used once before needing disposal. This one I found left in the wood near a discarded food wrapping.

"And, of course," the bear concluded, tapping the side of his snout, "these glasses."

The crow had seen the place where these cups were exchanged for money and translated, "Coffee," to the committee in the forest tongue.

"Coffee," the rest said in unison.

"So that is what the container is called?" the bear asked.

"It's just what I've heard."

"Riveting," said the bear. "I'll be sure to add coffee to my records."

When all gawking had concluded, the bear put his object back into the knothole from which it came, then officiated once again. "Alright, Crow. You've been patient and now it is your turn to present."

The crow cawed exuberantly and clawed the plastic bag he had brought with him. Then he feigned hesitancy. "I'm not sure if you're all ready for this."

"Yes we are!" croaked the frog.

"Let us see!" mooed the cow.

"Quit playing games," grumbled the bear.

"Alright," the crow teased, "prepare to be amazed!"

The crow flapped over with his white sack and out dropped a solid black block at the center of the ancient stump. When he landed he touched the tip of his beak to a silver bump on the side of the object. A source of light the same shape as its housing beamed upwards, scattering the curious fireflies. For a moment the bright white outshone their yellow glow, but eventually dimmed to a static image with some icons hovering above.

"Woah," said the frog.

"Woah is right," agreed the crow. "Raccoon, could you lend me a hand?"

"Me?"

"Yes. This device seems to respond to skin over claw, and you have the closest thing to thumbs out of the bunch."

Intrigued, the raccoon hopped up onto the stump and slowly approached the glowing thing. The white fur on his chin illuminated and his black eyes reflected the screen. The bear, slightly jealous, watched on quietly.

"Now," continued the crow, "could you press your hand to the little image that looks like a flower, but of every color."

The raccoon studied it for far too long before admitting, "They all look grey to me."

The crow tilted his head nearly ninety degrees, then tilted it back. "Oh, right. It's the only icon that resembles a flower, I suppose."

The raccoon saw one in the lower right-hand corner that he thought could be mistaken for a daisy and pressed his little thumb pad to it. On the screen, a grid of images filled the space where there were once foreign icons.

"Hey! That's our tree!" exclaimed the raccoon, noticing that the pictures were all of their Great Elm. "Look!"

The frog hopped up beside the raccoon, the bear and the

cow both leaned in closer, and the crow cleared his throat for a presentation. "Yes, this device can replicate the likeness of other things and then show them on its face, like butterflies and lizards. The humans call it a G-Phone."

However, the crow struggled translating "G-Phone" into the forest tongue because there was no existing word for it. He instead likened it to an artificial mockingbird. He did not feel guilty about this since he disliked mockingbirds deeply.

"So this . . . artificial mockingbird . . . steals our identities?" asked the bear. The rest were too preoccupied with the raccoon swiping through images of the Great Elm.

"And it does so much more!" added the crow. "Humans can use the phone to communicate with other humans who are anywhere in the world. It can play the songs of their kind. It can tell them things that they ask of it. And it also appears to distract them to dangerous degrees." *Just like the mockingbird*, the crow added internally.

"This is incredible," said the raccoon. An image of a large mushroom was now displayed and he was grasping for it with his little fingers. "It's as if it's there, but not there at the same time."

"And what level of human necessity does this mockingbird satisfy?" asked the bear with some edge to his voice. "Surely not as much as the coffee."

The crow did a small hop to turn towards the bear. "I bet you all the monies in Frog's mouth that a human would never leave one of these behind."

"Is that so?" challenged the bear. "Then how did you come by one?"

"I, like all crows, am a master of resourcefulness."

"So you stole it."

The crow took no offense. "Would you like to make this a wager?"

"I may. What are your terms?"

Tilting his head again, the crow said, "If you find one of these phones lying around, and bring it into our next meeting, I will preen your fur each day until the following moon."

"And if I cannot find one?"

"I would enjoy taking those monies home to my nest."

The bear thought for a while. He watched as the cow and the raccoon and the frog tapped on a different icon that displayed any human number they desired. If such a mockingbird could command the committee's attention so entirely and so effortlessly, then he did not want to bring another one anywhere near their Great Elm. "No deal."

"What!" squawked the crow. "But it's a harmless bet!"

The bear removed the human glasses and set them down on the stump. "Look at them, Crow. That device is not harmless. We need to dispose of it for the sake of the committee."

Now the infatuated trio had opened some sort of game where they were required to match colorful shapes together in groups. The crow could not find it within himself to disagree. He had witnessed humans so enamored with their phones that they would simply look over the friendly frog lapping up loose change, miss out on the rascally raccoon sorting through their trash, overlook the concerned cow watching them work the land, and disregard the benevolent brown bear cleaning up its forest.

"Fine," the crow said at last.

"Then it's settled," said the bear, nodding at the crow. "You know what to do."

The crow plucked the phone away from the trio to be put back inside the plastic sack. There was a mild groan from the committee, but it subsided quickly when the bear distracted them with his officiating.

"Right, back to business. Next moon. What should the topic of our scavenge be?"

After a few moments, the frog raised her glossy hand.

"Yes, Frog?"

"How about our favorite insects to eat?"

An even louder groan followed this suggestion.

"Come on, Frog," said the raccoon. "We already did that one, like, the second time it was the third time we'd done this."

"Are you sure? Because I recall it just being our favorite insects in general."

"How about the stinkiest thing from the trash?" offered the raccoon.

"Or the silliest piece of human clothing?" snickered the

cow.

The bear snorted at the bombardment. "Let's try and keep our themes informative, hm?"

"I'd say it's very important to know what stinks the most..."

And the squabbling sounds of the committee of curious collectors trailed the crow as he silently flew away from the Great Elm with a dangerously addictive device between his claws.

THE MOTHER'S EYE

Some stories are only as ambitious as the people who dare to tell them. History has not been kind to crude tales from shady sources, but this particular account, I suspect, had been purposely whittled down to a single dust-ridden diary and shelved for over 150 years. And while it may have been easier to regard this journal as the scribblings of a mad man, something about its proverbial yarn had been spun too tightly for me to discount it as mere fiction. The details were too . . . specific. Too consistent. Dates, locations, maps, sketches, names, all of them painted a complete and vivid picture of life from over a century ago. And all of them quietly led me to something even older . . .

How did I acquire such an enigmatic journal you ask? I assure you it was by complete mishap. You see, I was raised in the midwest of America and had always yearned to see the shrinking world. My first opportunity to travel abroad was an unpaid summer internship at the Maughan Library in London, England prior to my final semester of college. The position consisted of subservience, mostly to the tune of retrieving finished books from a bin and then returning them to their respective shelves. My shifts typically began in the evenings after the library had closed to the public. Perks were few, but I was able to explore London properly on most weekends.

One fateful night, while I was routinely shelving books in the lower archives, I accidentally bumped an unseen object with my elbow. It fell squarely between my feet, slapping the stone floor with a thwack! An old, withered thing bound by black leather looked up at me. I retrieved the peculiar object, lifting it carefully with both hands, and blew off decades of settled dust until it revealed a once-gold-lettered inscription: *Property of W. G.*

I opened it.

It took only a single page to learn that in my hands was a hand-written chronicle of 1800s America, and only two more before I was thoroughly charmed by its eclectic author. I read the journal from cover to cover, dusk 'til dawn, and then on each consecutive shift afterwards, obsessing over every detail of W.G. and his journey. Who was this man? Why had I never heard of him? And what exactly was this "Mother's Eye" he kept referring to?

When clues from the journal ran dry, I expanded my search to encyclopedias, historical archives, and even the internet, but found no mention of this man or his exploits. In fact, the text itself was not even registered in the Maughan's database. *Strange*, I thought, then, after numerous other libraries led me to the same dead end, I took my pursuit to the streets of London. I stopped in bookstores, colleges, city hall, and even the local pubs, but was only ever met with shrugs, scoffs, and shifting eyes. It became clear that my hunt for answers would need to continue much in the same way it had begun: alone.

So, at the end of my final shift, I pocketed the small ledger—knowing it would not be missed—and left with a mental compass of questions to guide my way. Then I spent the next five years of my life tirelessly piecing together what could quite possibly be the most unbelievable story you have ever heard.

JULY 13, 1850

The year was 1850 and America's east coast had been well industrialized. That summer, a man by the name of William Guinness was arriving in New York and the city was stirring with excitement. Guinness was a renowned explorer and, likely where he acquired most of his fame, a prolific debunker of legends, mysteries, and tall tales from all around the globe. For the first time ever he would be spending two weeks in the United States' largest city to share his latest discoveries in the form of ten conferences.

Being a master of his craft, there was not a single natural or man-made enigma that Guinness had not been able to expose. His events were advertised as the "Extraordinary Expedition of Worldly Explanations," but they were largely masked as an opportunity to exalt himself on the American people. Still, tickets to each seminar sold out in a matter of days and his audiences relished in his grandiloquence.

Between shows, a man like William Guinness could be found enjoying first class accommodations, first class dining, and first class suitors. Aristocrats who hosted Guinness would pay nearly a hundred dollars just to be seen in the same room as him. Guinness was a very tall and fit man who had a chiseled jaw and a thick head of sandy hair. He could always be found in his khaki explorer's outfit and was therefore easy to pinpoint in a sea of obese—and typically bald—American men in more ways than one. Guests would bombard Guinness with trivia they overheard from previous lectures such as, "Do the coffins really move in the Chase Vault?" or, "Did aliens actually build the pyramids?" and even, "Did the Mayans just vanish overnight?" However, Guinness was a professional, and he revealed nothing for free. He would only display his signature crocodile smile and tell them to purchase a ticket.

On the night of his final spectacle, July 13th, William Guinness strolled out to a sold-out theater flooded with press and wealthy fans. When the cheers halted he would pitch his favorite tagline: "Welcome to the Extraordinary Expedition of Worldly Explanations, where there's nowhere I haven't been and nothing I haven't seen!" The room would erupt until he motioned his hands downward, signaling the crowd to simmer. Over the next hour and a half he would display large photographs, maps, and documents of legends from every corner of the planet. His strategy was to hook the audience with a myth, then delicately follow up with hard evidence that proved there was never any wonder to begin with. He showed the crowd how Easter Island was once lush with trees until they were all cut down to be used as conveyors for giant stone faces, ultimately leaving the island uninhabitable. Then he told them how Stonehenge could have been erected by using simple lever and pulley systems. For the finale he would goad that the great pyramids of Giza were constructed using clever engineering and manpower without the need for any extraterrestrial assistance. To be frank, the tourist industry of the time hated William Guinness, but, luckily for him, taking advantage of others has always been profitable, especially in America.

After Guinness concluded his final presentation, he left his audience with one final thought: "And remember, if a story has been presented to you as myth or legend, know it to be false. There is always a rational explanation for everything." He then took a bow and walked off stage. The crowd sat bewildered at learning that so much of their pre-existing beliefs were only fabrications created by humans of the past. However, Guinness never cared if he caused any disappointment because he had already collected their money. Plus, he was setting sail back to his home in London early the next morning.

Once he pocketed his earnings from the box office, Guinness slunk out of the rear exit to avoid any fanatics and boarded his single horse-drawn carriage. It was approaching midnight and a cold fog sat low to the ground as he started for his hotel. During the ride he came upon the stone-laid street that led straight to his destination and noticed a blockage due to a crumbled building. *Odd*, he thought, because there was no such obstacle on his trip *to* the theater. It was no bother to him, however, because the roads of Manhattan were conveniently aligned to a grid, and he could just take the first left and then the first right.

The new road was considerably more cobbled and noticeably less illuminated. Guinness looked up at a nearby gas lamp and watched a breeze sneak through the cracked glass to extinguish its flame. Combined with the mist, the alley made Guinness slightly uncomfortable, for he knew that men in dark corners were far more frightening than stories of a Missing Link. But just as he ordered his horse to increase speed, a nut or a bolt dislodged itself from the rear axle bed and the seat detached from the cart.

"Of all damn nights for this cheap American . . . " he muttered under his breath.

Guinness hopped down and searched for the missing hardware, only it could not be found anywhere between the dimly lit cobbles. He looked around and weighed his options. The walk back to the hotel was roughly two miles and would take him maybe an hour to reach, but he was not thrilled about leaving his expensive supplies on the carriage. The other option was a small building across the street whose light just flickered on.

"The Frontier Saloon," Guinness read, squinting at the derelict sign hanging above the aging door.

Maybe, he predicted, help could be found inside. Surely men of the working class frequented such an establishment and any would jump at the opportunity to repair a celebrity's cart! And that was all the convincing Guinness needed to begin crossing the street.

As the Londoner entered the bar, he did not get the reaction that a man of his status was so accustomed to. There were no greetings, no smiles, no offers of free drinks, just eyes that would glance at him briefly, then turn away. Guinness also felt unsettled when realizing he was the minority in the room—in class and not of color—for the first time in years. Fortunately, he thought to himself, the bartender was a well-dressed Scotsman with slicked red hair and a complimenting mustache; someone familiar. Since standing around was making him stand out, he strolled over to his kind.

"What'll it be?" barked the bartender in his domestic accent.

"Excuse me my good man, my carriage broke down outside and—"

Before Guinness could finish, the Scotsman pointed to a small sign under a large mirror behind the bar that read "Paying Customers Only" in haggard handwriting. This offended Guinness. Not only was he not immediately recognized, but he had also not paid for his own drinks in over a decade! The look on the Scotsman's face was severe, though, so Guinness settled that he must have been unrecognizable under the pub's low lighting.

"Of course, my good man," Guinness swallowed. "I will have a glass of your finest Brandy."

"We got beer or whiskey," the bartender interjected, already irritated.

Suddenly more attuned to his environment, Guinness changed his order to the house whiskey. The bartender wiped the inside of a small tumbler with a stained rag he kept on his shoulder, grabbed one of only three green bottles under the "Paying Customers Only" sign, and filled the glass halfway. "One dollar," the bartender said, then immediately moved onto the next customer. Guinness had never felt so plebeian as he reached for his purse. He placed two dollars on the bar next to his glass and waited for the bartender's return so he could ask about the repair.

Nearly ten minutes expired when Guinness finally submitted to the water-stained glass half-filled with two-dollar whiskey sitting in front of him and took a drink. There was no distinct flavor of grain or barrel and his face cringed as he swallowed. When he opened his eyes, he caught a reflection in the mirror of a shadowy figure towards the back of the saloon. Something about the figure would not allow Guinness to break eye contact even though there were no visible eyes to begin with. Slowly, the shadow rose and lumbered towards the bar. Guinness broke his gaze and nervously attempted to leave his seat.

In a startlingly short amount of time, the figure occupied the stool next to William Guinness, reached over to his now quarter-filled glass of whiskey, and finished it for him. Guinness, frozen in place, did not know what to make of this oddity. Maybe it was an American jape he was not accustomed to. He knew a man of his stature was always tempting fate being around commoners, but did not feel in any clear danger at that moment. When Guinness finally turned to study the figure, he discovered it was a man of whose origin he had never seen before. The man had dark skin with a mahogany tint, a tall, curved nose that protruded from his brow, and strikingly long, braided black hair. He looked through heavy, almond-shaped eyes and wore unusually high cheekbones.

"That drink was only worth ten cents," the man jeered.

"It also tasted like it." Guinness could not place the man's accent as it sounded very foreign, yet simple, to him.

"You don't believe stories," the man said, looking forward and not at the celebrity to his right.

Guinness could not determine if that was a question or a statement, but answered anyway. "I believe everything can be proved or proven wrong," he said matter-of-factly. "There's nowhere I haven't been and nothing I haven't seen."

"I know of a place that cannot be and that you cannot see," the stranger countered, still looking forward.

"Then it cannot exist," Guinness replied, confident as ever.

"It is there. Always has been."

William Guinness paused for a moment. Of course he knew the bait was set to entice him, but he also had a ship to catch in the morning. He thought about the familiar offer for a moment and considered it almost certainly a ruse. Still, if something mysterious was out there it could mean another hefty payday. What he ended up saying was, "Show me this place and I will show you it has not."

"You do not believe?" the stranger jigged, waiting to set his hook.

"My good man, I will only believe what I cannot explain and, thus far, I have explained everything."

Quite a few events happened in The Frontier Saloon after he had said that. The overly arrogant statement must have struck a nerve with the dark stranger because he broke his gaze from the bar and looked directly at Guinness. The lights in the room dimmed to match the stranger's hair. The bartender and patron's movements seemed to halt, frozen in time. Guinness's stomach began to churn as he was pierced by the stranger's eyes and he started to believe just how sincere the man was.

"Far west from here, past the river Mississippi, there is a place where rushing water makes stone blush. A place within an endless sea of gold. A place with a mysterious wooden door. A door where you will discover the beginning of all time and, if you survive, where you will discover your true self."

Guinness chewed on that last statement for quite some time. This complete stranger could be lying or, even worse, could be telling the truth. The chance to expose such a curious door could potentially return profits he had never seen before; not to mention solidify his presence in the chapters of history books. Could he truly pass on such a gamble? At last, Guinness resumed the uncomfortable eye contact with the dark man and through his teeth he gritted, "My good man, you'll need to be more specific than that."

"That is the only way to find it."

William Guinness did not get this far in life by betting on impossible odds and the instructions given to him mirrored that of a needle in a haystack. Not wanting to reveal the scam was expected, but declining to reveal the scam's location? He had never heard such nonsense!

Since he was clearly not going to get the help he needed tonight, Guinness politely referred to the man as a fraud and admitted he would rather walk home than spend any more time among these delinquents. But as soon as Guinness stood up from his stool, the man grabbed his arm and got so close their noses touched. "Look for ones like me. Tell them you seek the door. Your eyes will be opened by hers . . . "

A shiver slid down Guinness's spine and when he shook the stranger's hand from his arm, the room returned to life. His nausea swiftly dissipated. He wanted to argue, but all he could muster was a, "Thank you . . . but good night, my good man," before he rushed towards the door. As his hand stretched for the knob he turned to ask one last question, but the dark stranger was nowhere to be seen.

"Say 'Hi' tae Nessie fer me when ye git home!" Guinness heard as he swung the door open, followed by resounding laughter. The handle latching behind him sealed off the ridicule and, in a way, his fate.

Almost simultaneously, the hanging fog had lifted and the soft glow of street lamps once again illuminated his carriage. Guinness immediately inspected the cart for the missing bolt and it appeared to be back in place, screwed tight. He then checked the gas lamp from before and the flame burned brightly. His gut mentioned something sinister about the repair, but his rationale told him that someone from the bar must have tended to it while he was being harassed. Either way, he rode back to his hotel without a second thought.

That night Guinness found himself tossing and turning,

unable to sleep for more than a short dream's worth at a time. What was peculiar to him was that each vision led to the exact same locations. He had a dream of himself in a wooden dinghy, completely lost inside an ocean of melted gold. Then he would be drowning in rapids surrounded by pink stone cliffs. Finally, he would turn the handle on a wooden door, only to wake up before the darkness revealed itself. Cold sweat saturated his sheets.

William Guinness packed at first light and, against all rationale and professional experience, started for the train station.

JULY 14, 1850

In the 1850s even a wealthy person such as William Guinness could not take a steam powered train directly to the heart of America. That railway simply did not exist. Instead he had to board one from New York to Buffalo, catch a ferry across Lake Ontario, board another train from Detroit to Chicago, and then commission someone brave enough to take him as far west as he needed.

After nearly five weeks of constant first-class travel, Guinness finally reached the end of the railway. At this time Chicago was a young city that envied New York as well as the people who migrated from it. And even though William Guinness did not call New York his home, he had just arrived from there, so he was not received as well as predicted. His fame also only stretched so far west which threw another unwelcome wrench in bargaining for transportation. It took three tedious days of haggling until he eventually came across a man named Birch—whom he referred to as 'simple enough'—who had a cart and two horses. Birch was the only one willing to make the trek into uncolonized territories with minimal details so long as Guinness paid up front in full. Guinness agreed, and they set out that same evening.

The second leg of Guinness's journey would be equally as long as the first. It was during these weeks he realized just how difficult his quest would become. Once they crossed the Mississippi river, the terrain decomposed from civilization in real time and Birch's cart was not equipped with state-of-the-art shock absorption.

To keep his mind from off his rattling spine, Guinness tried to explain the golden sea, the blushing rocks, and the mysterious, dark man as best as he could, but Birch only scratched his head and said, "I don't know nothin' 'bout no yella water, but I do know the whereabouts of some darker men."

That was the leading information Guinness had acquired thus far.

SEPTEMBER 23, 1850

Following extended weeks of travel, the days began to get shorter and the nights began to get colder. Guinness, who was used to traveling in the pillowed comfort of a private carriage, was growing irritated sitting on a wooden bench every day. On many occasions he thought of how his business partners across the Atlantic would laugh at his foolishness. How they would cut off his funding and distance themselves from his name. However, if the dark man from the bar was telling the truth, Guinness would not only become even more famous for discovering a mysterious door in the middle of the States, he would also be credited in all publications that followed. Just as Guinness managed a grin from his daydreaming, Birch spotted a camp at the base of a hill.

"We here, boss!" Birch said as he pulled the cart to a halt.

William Guinness sat up straight on the wooden bench and gasped at what he witnessed down below. He had experienced tribes who lived in huts, caves, and even elaborate tree houses, but he had never seen anything to this scale. Towering triangular tents supported by long, upright wooden posts created a circumference around the settlement. Scattered throughout were young men tending large wooden tanning racks with animal hides stretched across like pictures too small for their frames. In between, children chased each other and women prepared the remains of a hunter's kill. At the center of it all was an enormous fire blazing into the sunset sky, giving the appearance that one melted into the other. Nearby, even farther down the hill, strange hunchbacked cattle with thick fur and short, curved horns drank from a small bed of water. Guinness had never observed such primordial culture blending with such advanced civilization so seamlessly.

"They call 'emselves the Baxoje, but we call 'em the Ioways due to the state's name 'n all," Birch said while climbing down from the carriage. "Also, they don't speak no American."

"Then how will I ask them about the golden sea, the pink rocks, and the mysterious door?" Guinness replied with some panic lacing his tone.

"Don't worry yer shiny boots, boss. I know a word er two 'n I'll ask 'em. Jus' wait here."

Guinness shook his head, reclined against the stiff backrest, and waited for his guide to get them both killed.

While Birch chatted with what appeared to be an authoritative figure, there were many hand gestures aimed in Guinness's direction. Each time the tribesman looked towards Guinness he felt the price on his scalp increasing. After all, the American people did tend to refer to their tribes as savages...

Luckily, before Guinness's mind wandered too far, Birch came back to the cart.

"I got good news 'n bad news." Birch sighed.

Guinness predicted the bad news would include their hides and the massive open fire below. "The good news, please."

"The good news is they'll point ya in the right d'rection."

A sigh of relief. "And the bad news?"

"This is where we gotta part ways."

Guinness narrowed his gaze. "What do you mean, 'part ways'?"

"Y'ever rid a horse b'fore?"

"I am a world-famous explorer! Of course I've ridden a–"

"Well the chief says you can borrow one of they's horses, but he also says I ain't goin' with ya."

The Baxoje chief was now standing directly behind Birch and it became clear that the tribesman was at least a head taller than the both of them. This made Guinness even more uncomfortable. A deep sense in his bones similar to that of his last night in New York worked its way through his body. Whether a terrible mistake, or a promising next step, accepting this offer was the only way forward. Guinness climbed down from the cart and nodded at the chief.

The chief led Guinness to the pool of water he had seen upon arrival and approached a horse drinking alongside the wooly cattle. No words were said. The chief simply held out a rope that was tied neatly around the horse's neck. The steed was among the largest Guinness had ever seen and it did not come fixed with a saddle or stirrups.

"You must be joking," Guinness jeered. "A man of my caliber requires a custom fit saddle . . . "

The chief only grunted and motioned for Guinness to take the reins from him.

"Where is the golden sea? Where is the door? I need answers!" Guinness demanded, but the chief only furrowed his brow and shook the rope once again. There were a few moments of silent eye contact before Guinness succumbed and took the reins.

The first attempt at mounting the gigantic horse was that of a man too short to stand on one leg and swing the other one over. The next few attempts consisted of the same motion while adding an ambitious hop before each failed mounting. It was futile. And now that Guinness's embarrassment level matched that of his pride, the final attempt began to look something like a grown man trying to boulder up a horse's neck.

Stoically, the chief let out a precise whistle and the horse kneeled down to the ground. Guinness, still wrapped around the steed's broad neck, released and fell to the earth. He then stood up, baffled at how much power a man without a single dollar to his name seemed to have over him at that moment. Clearly Guinness was the butt of a joke to this tribe. But, as he straddled the kneeling horse, he felt that he would still have the last laugh.

The chief whistled again and the animal lifted as if it were hoisted by a crane. Guinness flung his arms around the horse's neck and held on tight, thinking he was about to be launched twenty feet into the air. Once he realized he was still on the steed's back, he looked down to the chief for instruction. The chief gazed towards the setting sun and raised an arm, index finger extended. Guinness's head turned to where the hand was pointed and slowly nodded. Then the chief struck the horse's haunch and it galloped away into the dying light.

SEPTEMBER 25, 1850

William Guinness and his newly-acquired horse traveled west overnight, the full day following, and all the way into that evening. How the animal could continue at speed for so long without rest, he had no idea, but fatigue was setting in on himself. The sun was settling on the horizon for the second time when Guinness felt his eyes getting heavy. Since the horse seemed to know where it was going, and showed no signs of slowing, he wrapped his arms around its neck and balanced himself so he could sleep.

As soon as Guinness began to drift, a startling object whizzed past his head, nearly taking an ear along with it. His eyes sprang open as the horse squealed and reared. Guinness attempted to get the huge animal under control, but another object zipped by his head, throwing him from his mount. The horse did not flee. Instead, it froze in place while Guinness frenzied on the ground, trying to reorient his bearings. Before he could see who—or what—had been after him, a single arrow pierced the dirt precisely between his thighs.

"Where did you get this horse?" a stranger demanded in darkness. "Thief!"

Guinness floundered and raised his fists. His eyes shot

left, then right, then left again, but still he could not find the stranger who had accused him. "This horse was given to me!"

The great horse shuffled, which startled Guinness, and then a tough leather bag shrouded his head. There was some movement at his extremities and he felt the burn of rope pull tightly against his skin. *One of the perks of the job*, he admitted to himself. But before he could squeeze out another thought, his legs were pulled out from under him and his head hit the cold earth.

It was the crackling warmth of fire that brought Guinness back to consciousness hours later. The leather bag had been removed and he was met with the eyes of twelve Natives sitting along the inner circumference of what he believed to be one of the giant tents he first saw a couple days ago. This council consisted of both men and women, all varying in age, and they sat eldest towards the middle with youngest on the ends. They all studied Guinness with inquisitive faces and he had a suspicion that they did not receive too many white visitors riding one of their horses.

"Thief," a stern woman addressed him. Guinness could now put a face with the voice that questioned him earlier. "How did you steal that horse?"

"It was given to me," Guinness disclosed, "by an Iowan man."

An angry young warrior rose to his feet. "We do not know of *Iowan*! Who did you steal it from, white thief?"

Guinness searched his memory for what Birch had called

the people in their native tongue and tried to reproduce it. "Apologies. Baxongee . . . Boxooje . . . maybe . . . Baxoje?"

This seemed to pique some interest among the group because the warrior sat back down, though reluctantly. A middle-aged woman spoke next. "And why would our Baxoje brothers and sisters give you their chief's great horse?"

"I don't know why it was given to me," Guinness fumbled, searching for the right words. "My guide spoke with the chief, then the chief gave me the reigns—"

The warrior slapped his hand on the ground, commanding the room once again. "The chief would never *give* his great horse to a *white thief* like you!"

"My good man," Guinness spoke somewhat too casually, "I had my guide inform the chief that I was looking for a wooden door, blushing rocks, and a sea of gold."

As the last word left Guinness's lips, the flame at the center of the great tent shrunk to a fragment of its original size and emitted a haunting blue glow. A dozen pairs of reflecting eyes moved around the room; gazing sometimes at each other and sometimes at himself. Guinness recalled having seen flame-changing powders during a stint in the Orient, but he had not seen anyone in the tent toss anything into the fire.

The eldest man at the center eventually broke the silence. "You seek the Mother's Eye?"

Guinness, concerned now more than ever for his safety, wanted to be absolutely clear with his words. "I'm not sure what it is I am seeking . . . or if it even exists. I was told by a man in New York to look for people like himself; to ask them about a place where rushing water makes stone blush. About an endless sea made of gold. About a wooden door.”

The flame continued to flicker pale blue as the council whispered among themselves. Guinness overheard them using a mixture of English and their native tongue. Within their argument he could make out words like, “thief,” and, “not worthy,” and, “banish him;” the latter making his skin crawl. Abandonment on wild territory inside a country he had never visited before was the last thing he needed. As thoughts crept down his spine and into his stomach, the eldest man in the center finally silenced the debate.

“You are not worthy to gaze into the Mother’s Eye,” he declared. “But you could not have stumbled across this knowledge by mistake. There is a reason it was revealed to you and we must honor that reason.” Guinness released a thankful sigh as the man continued. “Two of our own will guide you to the door. But be warned, stranger, you will not be the same man on the other side.”

The fire splashed back to its original color and size while the stern woman and the young warrior stood to approach Guinness. They each grabbed one of his arms and forcefully led him out of the tent’s entrance. He noticed it was still dark just before another leather bag covered his head. Both of his escorts spoke in unison: “Walk.”

It felt as if they had been traveling for an hour before

Guinness's guides said, "Stop." The escorts kicked the back of his knees so he would drop to the ground, then gave him a command to follow the water. There were no other instructions. The shroud was then removed from his eyes and he stood to look around.

Guinness found himself completely alone and it was nearly dawn.

SEPTEMBER 26, 1850

A deep blue sky speckled with twinkling stars illuminated an endless plain of wild grass. Aside from an occasional breeze or the distant trickle of running water, William Guinness wrapped himself in the vast silence. He closed his eyes and inhaled deeply. It was . . . calming.

His brief reverence soon came to a halt when a grumbling sound surfaced. His stomach. He had not consumed any food or water for over a day. These resources would need to be found soon and fortunately his instructions led him straight to one.

When Guinness reached the nearby source of water, he found that it was not simply a river, but a group of impressive falls. The black water barreled over the surrounding rock and crashed more than thirty feet below him, filling the air with a tingling mist. Excitedly, he ran down the hill and dipped his hands into the plunge pool for a fresh drink. It was so cold and crisp. At that moment he thought it was the best water he had ever tasted. After fully hydrating himself, he began the final search for something that resembled gold . . . or blush . . . or wood.

By now the sun had crept its way over the horizon and pushed a warmer hue over the land. Guinness appreciated the morning light, though it was still not bright enough to aid in his hunt. He had walked down and back up the entirety of the western bank and found nothing relating to his cryptic instructions. If anything interesting were to exist, he surmised it would most likely be near a memorable landmark such as the falls, so the next logical place to look was on the opposing bank. After careful consideration, he decided that the top of the waterfall would harbor the shallowest water in which to cross.

When Guinness reached the top of the hill, the sun was high enough to reveal small details in the water, rocks, and surrounding grasses. They all reflected the pinkish light of dawn which made it more difficult to see the riverbed. Still, he plunged his boot into the distorted water. It was shin-deep and just as cold as when he had tasted it. After a quick shiver, he began to cross the ford with large, deliberate steps and arms spread out for balance.

At around the midpoint, Guinness felt his boot sink between two rocks. This would have been easily avoidable had the sun been slightly higher, and he cursed himself for being so hasty, but he also knew that wallowing would only halt his advancement further. Calmly, he planted his free foot and leaned over to tug at his boot. He shook, wriggled, pulled, and pushed, but ultimately wedged himself deeper. Guinness, it appeared, was stuck.

Before giving up on his boot entirely, Guinness opted to try one more feat of strength. He crouched down low, shifted his weight, gritted his teeth, and pushed into the ground with all of his might. His boot popped free, but the effort sent him tumbling.

As the breeze steals seeds from a dandelion, so did the rushing water steal cries for help from Guinness's lungs. His body was tossed around silently as if it were made only of burlap and mulch. Each time he flopped down to a new terrace, his head plunged beneath the surface, completely disorienting his sense of up from down. He was a ragdoll trapped in a torrent. Once he plummeted over the last fall, he was sucked into the undertow and forced inside a small alcove on the eastern bank. The water in there swirled into a whirlpool, but Guinness was able to shore his battered body up onto a nearby ledge using his lengthy arms. Then he lost consciousness.

Guinness coughed back to life a few moments later. He found himself in a strange recess invisible to him earlier, surrounded by rocks adjacent to the lower falls. After spitting up a stomach full of water, he hunched up to his hands and knees and noticed something else peculiar. The misted stone he was encapsulated by displayed radiant shades of pinks . . . almost as if they were blushing. With renewed vitality he jumped to his feet and spun around to the most incredible sight that, to this day, few have ever been fortunate enough to witness.

The sun had fully broken through the veil of darkness to reveal a most magnificent dawn. The immeasurable amount of tumbling water created a glowing aura that refracted sunlight onto the pinkish rocks around them. The stone walls blushed through the misty haze in a way that could never be replicated by man-made palettes.

Guinness then gawked at what surrounded his vision further. Infinite miles of wild autumn grasses glistened in the breeze with the deepest saturation of gold he had ever laid eyes upon. East, west, north, and south, the grasses went on and on like a molten ocean. His brain could hardly process the enormity of such a display and his body reactively took a step back. Ironically, his same foot got wedged again, only this time it was not in between two rocks. It was a latch.

Guinness shook his foot free and gazed down at the mysterious handle that protruded from the ground itself. It was curious business that a metal ring would be lying on top of some overgrowth in the middle of nowhere, and it did not sit well with him. Puzzled, he wrapped both hands around the ring and pulled. A rectangular outline of grass and weeds stressed, then snapped to reveal what he had been searching for this entire time: a wooden door!

In a frantic state of adrenaline, Guinness pulled with enough force to break most of the natural seal. He then dropped to his knees, ripped the lingering vines from the edges, then returned to his feet to get a good look at his prize. He could not believe it. Lying before him was the wooden door housed by blushing stones within an endless sea of gold.

This must be the Mother's Eye! he thought to himself, grabbing the latch for a final time. *I am going to make a fortune!* Then he slowly peeled the door open to reveal...

"Stairs?"

To say that Guinness was disappointed would be an understatement. After months of travel, two encounters with cryptic Natives, and deciphering vague instructions from one place to another, his reward was a black hole hiding a stairway to nothing.

"Nothing here even remotely resembles a mother or an eye," he grumbled to the updraft of air escaping the opening. "And I don't even have a lantern to bring down with me."

Now that the sun was up, Guinness decided to climb to the top of a higher rock to catch his bearings. He saw that he could either follow the river until he reached another settlement, of which there was no guarantee, or risk venturing down into the hole. Alone. He rubbed his empty stomach and decided he had enough fuel left in his tank to briefly explore the hatch.

Guinness hopped down and peered into the hole with his hands resting on his thighs. The sun was directly above now. As long as he left the door open, he should be able to reach the bottom safely using the overhead light. So he took a deep breath and tested the durability of the first step. It was as firm as the surrounding rock and, oddly enough, constructed of the exact same type of pinkish stone. *Whoever had made this staircase,* Guinness acknowledged while gathering his confidence, *had done so with craft.*

Finally, Guinness descended into the darkness.

Each flight contained exactly ten steps before turning ninety degrees to the next flight. This went on and on for as far as the eye could, or could not, see. There was no railing so Guinness was extra cautious not to fall into the center—one tumble would be enough for him that morning.

Step after step after step led him further into the Earth and farther away from the sun. He paused to rest for a moment, still hungry, still fatigued, and observed how far he still had to go. Even after his eyes had adjusted to the darkness, there was no end in sight.

When Guinness regained some stamina, he wiped his brow with a dirty rag from his pocket and continued down until the dwindling light barely outlined his hand in front of his face. *This is enough,* he gritted, *I need to use what's left of my strength to get home in one piece. I will document the location and bring an excavation crew in a few weeks' time.* Without a second thought, he turned around to climb back up the stairway only to witness his one source of light being extinguished. "Damn."

With one arm bracing the wall and the other held out for balance, Guinness grumbled to himself how he should have placed a rock on the door so the wind could not accidentally close it. He worked his way back to the top and pushed on the hatch. It was sealed tight. He pushed and slammed and beat on the door further, but it did not give at all. Guinness was a tall and strong man so he found the amount of resistance a bit ridiculous. So as a last ditch effort, he squatted down on the third step, placed his hands on the door, and pushed upwards with all the might his body could provide. The door flexed to reveal a sliver of light, but ultimately held tight.

Guinness took a few deep breaths. His good fortune had ebbed and flowed too unpredictably on this venture. Had he trapped himself inside the very thing he sought after all these months? No. He would prove himself the victor in this absurd and wild goose chase. Guinness clenched, grunted, and pressed into the hatch's underbelly with his entire might. The strain against his already-bruised bones was unbearable. His worn boots dug and dug into the ancient step until there was a sudden *crack!*

A section of stone separated from the staircase, pulling a man along with it into the depths.

Guinness screamed until he was out of breath, filled his lungs, then screamed again. He kept tumbling and tumbling, trying to orient himself or grab onto something protruding from the wall. There was nothing but nothingness. He eventually wriggled his body to the point where he thought he was plunging headfirst—a slight improvement. It was not until then did Guinness build up the courage to open his eyes, but what he witnessed stole the charge from every nerve inside his body. Limp, he stared into the abyss, and the abyss stared into him.

When the shock wore off, Guinness's nerves began to fire again. He realized that he seemed to be falling at a faster rate every second, yet there was almost no resistance in the air. Usually, no resistance meant no air, and he wondered if he would suffocate before he hit the bottom. Then he thought about actually hitting the bottom; ensuring a horrible death either way. The folds in Guinness's brain began to wriggle for answers. Who could dig such a chasm? What purpose does it serve? Where does it lead? But as the grip on reality continued to slip, so too did Guinness's consciousness.

At least he thought he had blacked out. The absence of light mixed with the acceleration of gravity can corrupt even the strongest of minds. Guinness began to feel things that once only danced at the edge of his psyche. It felt as if he was growing taller, yet shrinking at the same time. His flesh and bones were stretched in every imaginable direction while simultaneously compressing back into his body. His mind unfolded and wrapped him in a chrysalis of self-awareness. He was William Guinness, and William Guinness was him.

A warmth penetrated soon after. Not the heat of a sun, but a new form altogether. It could be seen by the blind, heard by the deaf, felt by the numb. It radiated from deep within, absorbing Guinness completely. Then his mind retreated. He could no longer think. No longer see. No longer breathe. No longer feel. Cosmic forces took hold of him, swallowed him, and spat him back out. At last, William Guinness was nothing.

Then, strangely enough, the inconceivable carnival ride began to slow down just as quickly as it had sped up. Not by much, but Guinness could *feel* that he was no longer at terminal velocity. This welcome deceleration allowed his brain to form thoughts once again, to be in control of itself. Now he could focus on not being flattened by whatever waited for him.

But slower and slower and slower Guinness fell until he was nearly stagnant . . . weightless . . . floating. *Is this just some delusion of fatigue and hunger?* he wondered. It did seem the likeliest answer, especially when his head thumped into something firm.

"The hatch!"

Not willing to miss his chance at freedom, Guinness flailed his arms at the obstruction above until his hands brushed against a metal ring, confirming his intuition. *I must have passed out from overexertion while trying to open it earlier!* Thinking quickly, he clasped both hands around the latch and held on for dear life.

But something was different about the hatch now. Was it the temperature? The barometric pressure? The ambient sounds of nature outside? Suddenly, Guinness heard a new *thump!* from above, followed by a man's grunt. Guinness gulped.

Silence...

The hatch swung open, pulling Guinness's depleted body out with it! His tired grip released and he landed face-first on something soft.

"Forty two minutes flat. That is a new record!"

A bright source of light blinded Guinness as he rolled onto his back. "Where...where am I?"

"You are on the other side!" the voice exclaimed.

Guinness's blurred senses could only make out a dark silhouette and the familiar noise of rushing water. Only now the water sounded more like crashing waves and less like tumbling falls.

"Who are you?"

"You do not recognize me?"

Guinness's eyes were still tender. The mysterious figure slowly morphed into a defined shape, revealing auburn features and long black hair.

"Ah, you cannot see. A typical side effect after seeing the Mother. Let me give you a hint: 'that drink was only worth ten cents.'"

"Y...you're the man from the Saloon?" Guinness was frantically exhausted. "What was that thing? What have you done to me!"

"Easy now. Take deep breaths," the man encouraged. "You just looked into the Mother's Eye and lived to tell about it."

Guinness's own eyes were now fully contracted and he

could finally see the man, but that was not what demanded his attention. The golden grasses, the pink rocks, and the misty falls were all gone. He was sitting in the middle of a rocky beach watching ocean waves crash into a shoreline. "Where in the hell am I?"

"Most call this Kerguelen Island. It is north of Antarctica, somewhere in between Madagascar and Australia."

"Less than an hour ago I was in the middle of the United States!" Guinness snapped. He stood to his feet, wobbled, faltered, "How did I...how did we...where did we," then fell to his knees. His body and spirit were completely drained.

"Now do you believe?"

Shortly after, the man known only as the mysterious stranger from The Frontier Saloon lifted Guinness to his feet and ushered him onto a small tugboat. The stranger promised to take Guinness to the nearest port and told him they would never see each other again. They were at sea for a few days. During that time Guinness rationed, swore, agreed, disagreed, and yelled at himself. No matter how much he brainstormed, or how much he twisted his own truth, he could not come up with an explanation for what had happened to him. It rotted him to the core.

When they reached port in Madagascar, the dark stranger placed a small purse of money into Guinness's palm and closed his fingers around it. Before releasing his grip he stared deeply into Guinness's eyes and gave some parting advice:

"If you look for it, you will never find it."

Of course, the first thing William Guinness did was try and find it.

After arriving home in London he sought to convince his business partners of the Wonder in the West—as he failed to coin it—and reiterate just how much money could be made from such an attraction. He vehemently explained to them that cryptic Native Americans lent him a giant horse, sent him galloping for days without rest, attacked him with arrows, bagged his head, turned fire blue, led him to a golden ocean, and tricked him into entering a hatch that tunneled all the way through the center of the Earth. They would be millionaires, he cheered. Millionaires!

Unfortunately, Guinness's exuberant retellings came across as utterly unbelievable, and unprofitable, to the tempered businessmen. Not to mention dangerous. Instead of unyielding support, they decided their explorative partner would benefit more from an indefinite hiatus. This would give Guinness time to recover from whatever happened across the Atlantic, and them time to draft the separation agreement. And just like that the renowned, handsome, and boisterous host of the Extraordinary Expedition of Worldly Explanations began another endless fall; this time from grace.

The next bit will likely come as no surprise to seasoned explorers.

William Guinness spent his final years and his entire bank

account trying to relocate the Mother's Eye. He searched all over the Midwest to pinpoint the Natives he had once encountered, but the American landscape was changing, and it was changing fast. The Midwest rapidly developed with settlers from the East Coast and the original landmarks grew more and more difficult to distinguish. Continuation of this Westward Expansion displaced the native people who had shown Guinness the Eye from their former territories and onto reservations. Guinness even tried tracking down Birch in Chicago only to discover that he moved away after striking a "big ol' payday from some crazy Brit."

Guinness's fame withered as fast as his fortune. No one in America would believe his proclamation and eventually stopped listening altogether. His hair grew long, his beard grew mangy, his teeth stained brown, and his mind began to decay with obsession. During his later years bad health rendered him unfit for exploration and ultimately forced him to relinquish his quest. Until his untimely death in 1867, William Guinness was said to be found drinking ten-cent whiskey at The Frontier Saloon in New York City.

1870

While this would effectively bestow a fitting end to the tragedy of William Guinness, it gives no justice to the Mother's Eye. What became of it? Where was it? What was it? Had it even existed?

While I flipped through the final pages of W.G.'s tattered journal, the descriptions and sketches of the Eye's location rang eerily similar to a thriving park in my hometown of Sioux Falls, South Dakota. At what is now known as Falls Park, there are multiple waterfalls totalling roughly 40 feet high and they are surrounded by the State's indigenous "blushing" rock, Sioux Quartzite. The fields of wild grasses have long since been replaced with buildings, streets, and walkways, but they would not be difficult to imagine.

All of these similarities, locations, and coincidences could no longer be ignored. My eagerness for answers led me deep within the Sioux Falls public archives. For weeks I studied dusty pages long forgotten. Then one fateful night, to my utter astonishment, I discovered this legend had a fraternal twin . . .

In the spring of 1870 another prestigious individual discovered the Mother's Eye, only this time by accident. A man by the name of Richard F. Pettigrew pioneered the development of a small town in southeastern South Dakota which changed his life forever. While surveying the area for what would later be named Sioux Falls, he stumbled across a distinctive door on the eastern bank of the Big Sioux River. It was covered in vines. He opened it.

At first Pettigrew wanted to hire a team to explore what lay below the hatch, but decided to keep it to himself once he noticed the vines resealing the door every single day. Over the course of a week he noted that growth would happen precisely when the sun was at its highest in the sky; strange business for anyone spelunking before noon. He continued to document in secret and began timing his own explorations with the closing door, but never got far enough down to satisfy his yearning. That is until one morning where he also slipped and fell into the void.

Pettigrew traveled all the way through, bumped his head on the other side, and then, unaware of an opposing handle to clutch onto, fell all the way back to his original location before noon. Once safely outside of the Midwestern hatch he crawled a generous distance and watched the vines reclaim the wooden door. That night he tossed and turned and sweated and screamed. The horror of that journey combined with the fact that, had he entered the hatch just minutes later he would have been trapped in an eternal freefall, robbed him of any sleep for weeks. Eventually he resolved that such an inexplicable hazard below the foundation of the very town he was trying to pioneer simply would not do, and he vowed to cover up that hatch at any cost.

1879

After years of toiling, Richard Pettigrew devised the perfect plan to eliminate anyone from ever discovering the mysterious hatch while still advancing construction on his beloved town. He would commission a towering, seven-story flour mill on top of the perilous trap door and use the nearly-indestructible Sioux Quartzite as a seamless foundation. Such an ambitious building would be functional, draw tourism, and seal off a dark secret forever. Despite careful planning, Pettigrew still found that his primary obstacles were lack of funding and lack of water. He knew the depth of the Big Sioux River could never support a mill of that magnitude, so he needed to be clever. He needed a scheme.

Months later, Pettigrew used what money he had left to hire young, uneducated men to dam the Big Sioux upstream from the falls. Then he told the men he would sweeten the pot if they conveniently destroyed the dam just before his investors from New York arrived to inspect the location for the mill. The men thought this slightly unethical, but they also agreed that money was money and no one was getting hurt. As ordered, the men built and then destroyed the dam a few weeks later, which temporarily raised the water level by over a foot. The investors were so impressed by the power of the mighty Big Sioux River and its falls that they immediately funded Pettigrew's massive pink project.

The Queen Bee Mill was constructed later that year.

TODAY

Of course, as modern history has it, the water level quickly subsided and the mill only churned from 1879 to 1881 before it had to be shut down for good. In 1956 an all-consuming fire destroyed the complex and all that remains of the Queen

Bee is its rosy foundation. However, Richard Pettigrew's mill had and still serves its underlying purpose: Completely sealing off the Mother's Eye for well over a century.

Years of my young adulthood were spent obsessing over what was fact and what was fiction. Were they wasted? I'm not sure. Even today I find myself jogging the trails through Falls Park from time to time. I stop, admire the waterfalls, cross the bridge, climb the rocks. But before leaving I always find myself standing at the base of the Queen Bee Mill's remains. Now there's just a small, arched gate blocking off the area underneath. One could easily slip through the space created by a missing beam in the doorway, but a string of chain and a padlock wards most would-be trespassers away.

I went in once. I crawled through the gap just to see if mother nature would graciously confirm my findings. I dropped to my hands and knees, leaned my head to the dirt, and listened for anything out of the ordinary. All was quiet except for the rushing water outside. But then, roughly around the center of the area, I assure you I heard a faint thump directly below my ear. A thump that eerily resembled a skull connecting with a rotted wooden door.

BO×ES

In a land where everyone carries around their misery, doubt, and hardships inside a box, very few can look up to notice others. Some boxes are small, some are larger, some are near empty, and some are so full they need to be hefted on one's back. Because of these boxes, shame threatens those who ask for help, and punishes those who offer it. Solace can only be found in keeping to oneself.

Noah did not have a box. Every day he walked the streets watching the people look down at their own, wondering why they were the ones to be with, and he was the one to be without. He did not know what those boxes contained—did not care—he just knew that he wanted it. To him having a box was unfair, and he was lonely.

One day Noah decided it was time to learn why everyone else carried a box while he did not. He spotted a young girl across the street struggling with hers, so he conceived a plan and ran over to speak with her.

"Little girl," he said. "I noticed your box looks too heavy. Can I help you with it?"

The girl's clothing was tattered and her face was stamped with a permanent frown. It was as if she had never experienced joy in her entire life. She looked up at Noah with surprised eyes. No stranger had ever talked to her, let alone offered their hand.

"Wh . . . where's your box?" the girl asked.

"I don't have one," Noah replied. "That's why I want to help you carry yours."

For a few moments the girl hesitated. For as long as she could remember she had always carried her own box. Then again, no one had ever told her she could not give it to someone who asked. "Here, you can just have mine. I'll get another one somewhere else."

Thinking himself clever, Noah grinned and reached out to receive the young girl's box. Immediately a swarm of sadness rushed over him like an icy tide. He saw the girl seated by an empty hospital bed. Her mother had succumbed to illness. At home her father turned to dark bottles of resentment. The house became dark and cold and lacked every piece of the warmth and love that Noah was accustomed to.

"You've been carrying this around your whole life?" he asked.

"Been carrying what?" she replied.

"The memory of your—"

Noah stopped himself because he suddenly realized what all of the boxes contained. What they meant. That he had just inadvertently lifted a lifetime of suffering from a young girl's shoulders.

"I don't know about a memory, but that thing sure was heavy!"

Then the girl giggled, perhaps for the first time in her life, and she said thank you. Noah smiled back. To him, her bright expression far outweighed anything that could be shoved into a box.

"Well, I've got it from here," he told her. "You go run along and play."

And from that day forward, if Noah ever saw anyone struggling with their box, he offered to carry it.

DESTINATION EARTH

PART II

Click. Click. Click. Click. Whhhurrrrrr.

"Coordinate four-five-one-six contains no anomalies. Moving to next sector."

Click. Click. Click. Click. Whhhurrrrrr.

"Coordinate nine-nine-seven-two contains no anomalies. Moving to next sector."

Click. Click—

"Jensen, do you have to say every single coordinate out loud?" Colonel Prack interjected, slamming his newspaper on the table. "It's three in the damn morning and I'm trying to catch up on this godforsaken water conflict in Europe."

May Jensen peeled her eye from the viewing lens of the Greenburg-Sahara Telescope and sighed. "It helps me focus so I don't lose my place. You don't want us to have to start over, do you, sir?"

"Yeah, yeah, get on with it."

Click. Click. Whhhurrrrr.

"Coordinate one-nine-two-four contains no anomalies. Moving to next sector."

Click. Click. Click. Click. Whhhurrrrr.

"Coordinate eight-one-seven-one contains no anomalies. Moving to next . . . wait a second."

"Hm?" the colonel grunted without looking up from his article.

Jensen did not elaborate. Instead, she lightly rotated the focusing dial left and right until she was sure she was not mistaken. She was not. A microscopic burst of light had appeared almost directly opposite the sun and then flickered out. What remained was a small, dark, spherical object that vibrated uncontrollably.

Jensen yanked her head from the viewing lens and checked her glasses for flecks or smudges. They were spotless. She then considered the natural fatigue of an overnight shift so she rubbed her groggy eyes before peering back through the telescope.

"Uh, colonel, you should come take a look at this."

Crinkling the edges of the newspaper with irritated fists, the colonel huffed, "It's the same sky every night, Jensen. Just mark it down and move on."

"There's . . . um . . . something out there. S . . . something new."

"Spit it out already," the colonel said after taking the time to sip his coffee first. "You're acting like you've seen a goddamn flying saucer."

Jensen did not want to peel her eyes from the lens, but she needed confirmation from a superior that she was neither delirious nor sleep-deprived. Either way she could not explain to him what was happening in the nearby vacuum of space. "I don't know what it is, but it wasn't there a few minutes ago."

"A leaf probably blew on the lens. The wind'll get it soon."

"Not a leaf, sir," she corrected without reminding him that they were on top of a mountain in the middle of New Mexico. "It's growing."

Colonel Prack slid back his chair, stood, and strolled heavy-shouldered to the viewing platform. Jensen exited her seat and invited him up the small staircase to test his eye. "This better be good," he said as he took off his hat and leaned in. He only gazed for a brief moment before turning back to Jensen unamused. "You think playing jokes at three in the morning is funny, Jensen? I know Mercury when I see it."

"What? No, I..." Jensen was taken aback. The object she was talking about was not even in the same field of view as

Mercury, not to mention one millionth its size. "Let me see that again."

Visibly agitated, Colonel Prack grumbled and got up from the viewing chair. Jensen swooped in immediately, touched her glasses to the lens, and adjusted the focus. The colonel had already started back down the stairs when he heard, "This . . . this is impossible. It was no larger than a basketball a few moments ago. Now it's a planet!"

The colonel spun around mid-step and gripped the railing. He made sure to speak clearly and concisely. "You mean to tell me that that thing is *not* Mercury, Venus, the moon, or any other known object in our solar system?"

"Correct," Jensen replied, running some hasty measurements in her head. "There's no probable way it could be. It's exactly the same distance from the sun as Earth, and in exactly the same orbital plane."

Colonel Prack's knees suddenly felt weak. He was glad he still had his hand on the rail. "Jesus! Where did that . . . that *thing* come from? Is it going to hit us? What does NASA do in this situation?"

"Situation? Sir, this isn't even on our list of things to *begin* brainstorming about!"

Ignoring the colonel while he stroked his mustache and muttered his expletives, Jensen went back and forth between the viewing lens and her notepad, jotting down every minute detail she could identify. But how did one describe a rapidly expanding cosmic object? After all, she went to school for numbers, not for words. She bit the tip of her pen in thought, then wrote in all sincerity:

The anomaly behaves like a timelapse of a blooming dahlia, only the petals are made up of trillions of grains of sand, and the granules continue to orbit the pistil until collapsing to the surface under the object's ever-increasing gravitational pull.

Jenen bit the tip of her pen again. She felt what made it to paper did the anomaly's poetic brilliance no justice, so she jotted down a few more trailing thoughts:

Pulsating jellyfish...
Contained, spherical explosion of dust...
Food coloring dropped in hot water...

After the last mark she conceded to continue observing.

For a moment the object seemed to reach a catalyst because it stopped increasing in size and the orbiting sediment had all settled on the surface. Then, after Jensen looked away for the briefest of blinks, she returned to find bright red veins sprawling across the object's hardening crust. Magma. Which meant volcanoes. Which meant, "Cripes! Come look at this now!"

Colonel Prack snapped from his spouting and slipped eagerly back into the chair. "Looks like a bunch of yellow gas. Methane, maybe?"

"What?" They swapped again and Jensen could hardly swallow her excitement. This was the type of discovery scientists only dreamed about dreaming about. "More like the formation of an atmosphere!"

They switched places dozens of times as gas condensed around the anomaly. Lightnings crashed and winds began to shape clouds. Soon the red veins turned to billowing steam as harsh rain violently cooled the surface. All the while the clock ticked.

"Alright, we need to think, and we need to think fast," Colonel Prack assessed nervously. "Who else can see this thing?"

Jensen quickly diverted her eye to check the watch around her wrist. "Just us. We have an exclusive field of vision until oh-nine-hundred."

"It's nearing six now. We should notify the big wigs about this."

"No," Jensen said matter-of-factly. "Extraordinary claims require extraordinary evidence. We need to have a grasp on what we're witnessing, however weak that may be. Besides, this . . . planetoid . . . is developing too rapidly to waste precious seconds on phone calls. Look, now!"

Colonel Prack raised an eyebrow at the near-insubordination, but he knew Jensen was right. There was simply too much happening too fast. When the two switched spots again the colonel's jaw dropped. "Is that...?"

"An ocean? Yes!"

"And are those...?"

"Yes!" Jensen had not been this excited since the James Webb Space Telescope took its first photograph of outer space. "Plants!"

The colonel slouched back in the viewing chair, as if mesmerized. He dabbed some sweat from his brow and pulled his hat back over his thinning hair. Concentrating during quite possibly the most important revelation in human history was near impossible. "What does this look like to people on the ground?"

Jensen was already leaning over the colonel so as not to miss a single moment. "Civilians? This isn't a popular season for stargazing. Unless someone has a telescope and is looking at this specific spot, it will look like a shadow to the naked eye."

"Alright, Jensen," Colonel Prack mused while stroking his mustache again, "I'll need you to constantly monitor this thing until oh-nine-hundred rolls in and all hell breaks loose. Bark at me for anything you need to stay awake and focused. Use every piece of hardware we have to record that thing and write down everything else in between. In two-and-a-half hours, I'll have no choice but to make the call."

Minutes rolled by as briefly as seconds and the colonel had just ground the beans for their fourth consecutive pot of coffee. Aside from the potential court-martial he would face for delaying the single greatest discovery in the history of mankind, his only worry was to keep May Jensen documenting efficiently and effectively. The importance of her work in these few short hours was paramount, and their combined diligence was the correct course of action. Perhaps their only way to prepare for the worldwide panic to come.

Colonel Prack then began to dread the announcement he would inevitably have to make. Not the one to the higher-ups, but to the public. The average civilian would certainly see him as complacent in another government conspiracy and global tensions were high enough as it was. Water conflicts in Europe. Oil conflicts in the Middle East. Humanitarian conflicts in Asia. Political conflicts in the States. This was *not* the time for something so existential to pop out of the sky.

Then, just as he pressed "brew" on the coffee machine, he heard, "Colonel, come quick!"

He ran back into the viewing room as fast as his legs would carry him. "What is it!" he yelped, nearly out of breath.

Jensen hesitated. "Something different is happening now. It's . . . slowing down."

"What's slowing down?"

"The, um, evolution." She paused, choosing her next words carefully. "It's tapering off. Natural formations, vegetation, animals . . . they're stagnant. I'm no biologist, but it's almost like the planet has reached an equilibrium. Like it caught up to where it's supposed to be. Like it was before."

"Before what?"

Jensen chewed on the edge of her pen. "I'm not sure."

"Let me have a look at that."

Jensen slid over once again for the colonel. He found that this time it was more like looking into a mirror instead of a telescope lens. Vast mountain ranges, dense forests, great oceans . . . they were all there just as they were on Earth, only more full, more lush. His heart drummed with anxiety. What did it all mean?

Then the colonel spotted something even more peculiar. On the darker edge of the planet there was a blip of warm light. "How far can this thing zoom in?" he asked, and Jensen quickly adjusted some parameters to digitally enhance the window. "That's about as far as it goes," she said.

"Ho. Lee. Shit." The colonel began shaking in his seat. "You *won't* believe this."

May Jensen swapped with him and leaned her head over the lens. She gasped. A large fire burned inside the safety of a deep valley surrounded by mountains. It wasn't a natural fire, however, since it was contained by a circular arrangement of stones. Positioned around the flame appeared to be logs, but flattened, or cut in half long-ways to resemble benches. Then she saw them. From a nearby cave, a single person stepped into the light. Followed by another. And another. And another. And another until thirteen human beings sat down on the benches around their campfire.

In the other room the coffee machine beeped, reminding Colonel Prack to look at the time. "Jensen," he said.

"One second."

"Jensen," he sighed. Heavily. "It's nine o'clock."

NGOZI RUFU

ALL YOU CAN EAT

Deep in the heart of Zimbabwe there lies an empty field of clumpy grasses and bushy trees. A field that has not known human footsteps in decades, but is still littered with their eroding bones. Along one side, far away from civilization, stands a forgotten fence. The fence is crude, consisting of wooden posts tied upright with spans of mangled barbed wire. And right at the center of this fence's length stands a single steel sign serving a single salient purpose: warning passersby not to enter. A warning that two perched vultures were trying desperately to decipher.

"I'm telling you Zira, those are *bones* on the sign. It

means food for us."

"Are you and I even looking at the same thing? It's a *human* skull and bones, Tongai!"

Zira and Tongai both stretched out their wings as far as they could go to emphasize how much they were right, and the other was wrong. They hopped up and down, bobbed their long naked necks, and hissed at each other with great conviction. Finally, Tongai took flight and landed on top of the steel post that housed the enigmatic sign.

"Look, Zira," he said as he tapped on the image with a single claw. "Humans always put up signs in front of places they eat. Why else would they paint it this pretty red color?"

Zira fluttered over to the nearest post to make her point. "You're such a bird brain!"

Tongai puffed out his chest feathers and brought his wing over as if he was straightening a necktie. "I take that as a compliment."

"Well, you shouldn't!" Zira said quickly to squash Tongai's ego. "Everyone knows humans use red as their danger color."

"Then answer this if you're so smart: why would they scribble 'all you can eat' on either side of the bones if it wasn't an advertisement for free food?"

"You can't read human writing, Tongai. Don't even pretend you can."

In the midst of the Vultures' squabbling, a lone animal walked into the field of clumpy grasses and bushy trees and started nibbling on the brush.

"Sh, sh, sh, sh, sh!" Tongai whispered. He hurriedly flapped to the post next to Zira's and spread a silencing wing across her beak. "Look! A wildebeest!"

A nip would have done it, but instead of suffering the aftermath of a known complainer, Zira just shoved Tongai's rude gesture away. The two watched on as the huge animal moved from bush to bush filling its stomachs. It did not notice the two spectators, but would not have cared if it did. No live animal ever feared a vulture.

"*See*," Tongai interjected. "Food!"

Zira rolled her bulbous eyes and mocked Tongai. "What are we supposed to do? Wait for it to eat itself to death?"

"Just trust the sign, Zira."

Nearly half an hour passed and the wildebeest showed no signs of ending its graze. It would chew off every leaf from one bush, mow down some of the patchy grass, then find some other untouched cluster of green to nibble on. After what seemed to the vultures to be the hundredth and final morsel for the beast, it moved on to its hundred and first. Only this time, after a few steps, there was a snappy *click!* followed by an enormous blast.

Tongai and Zira flapped backwards from the shock and fell into the grass below. On the ground they heard a variety of *splats!* followed soon after by the intoxicating aroma of fresh blood. The new promise of fresh food immediately suppressed any fear the vultures may have suffered and they flapped back up to the posts they had been perched on.

"What did I tell you?" Tongai gloated as chunks of wildebeest still rained from the summer sky. "Free food!"

"I'll be damned. It *does* say 'all you can eat'!" Zira yapped with her beak wide open. She motioned to hop down from the fence, but Tongai yet again spread out his wing.

"Hold up. Now I don't know what kind of human voodoo is going on here, but we should probably *fly* to where the food is. I don't want to end up like our meal."

Zira watched the final chunk of wildebeest get caught on a branch and shuddered. "Right. Good call."

For the remainder of the afternoon the two vultures flew from piece to piece of the easiest feast they had ever plunged their heads inside. There were no predators, no humans, and, best of all, no other vultures to swoop in on their prize. They filled their bellies until not a morsel remained, then flew back heavy-winged to the vulture tree for the best night's sleep they had ever had. But before drifting off completely, they vowed to one another that they would never tell another soul about their secret buffet.

This went on for months until Tongai and Zira were so plump they could barely make the flight home to the vulture tree. They would sneak away from the flock in the morning, perch upon the posts, and wait for unsuspecting ungulates to explode into prepped meals. For them, it may as well have been vulture heaven.

"What do you think'll show up today?" Zira asked.

"Is it weird to say I'm sick of wildebeest?" Tongai replied. "I hope it's an antelope. Ooh, or a zebra!"

"Ooooh, zebra *would* be delicious." She licked her beak, then cocked her head towards Tongai. "Say, do you think it's about time we told the others?"

"About what?"

"*This*, you bird brain!"

"Absolutely not!" Tongai was shocked and showed it by pressing his wingtips to his chest. "This was our discovery. Well, *my* discovery."

Zira ruffled the feathers around her neck. "What do you mean *your* discovery? We were out here at the same time!"

"Sure, but it was *I* who read the sign."

"We both know you still can't read human, Tongai."

"Can too!"

The two had fallen back into their pattern of grunting and wing-spreading when the familiar sound of flapping came within earshot. Zira and Tongai swiveled their long necks and saw an incoming nuisance. "Great," Zira hissed. "Woody's here."

Like an uninvited third wheel, this new vulture took his perch between the two squabblers. "Well howdy-do Zingai! Whatcha up to?"

"Zingai?" Zira asked without saying hello.

"It's what I been callin' you two since you're always hangin' out together. Zira and Tongai equal Zingai! Get it?"

"Fascinating," Tongai hissed. "What are you doing out

here?"

"Oh, I was gettin' tired of rustlin' with the others so I decided to get up early and surprise you two!"

"Well, Woody, we didn't ask you to come with us," Zira grunted.

"I know!" Woody chuckled. "That's why it's a surprise!"

Tongai was scowling at their happy-go-lucky intruder. "How did you even wind up here from America, anyway?"

Woody extended his long neck up like a spring of excitement. "Oh, that's a great story! It all started after I chased some wily mice onto a *really* big boat—"

Tongai was not about to listen to Woody's autobiography so he quickly interrupted. "Save it. Can't you see we're busy?"

"Ya'll don't look that busy," Woody observed, "but I will go ahead and save the best part of the story for supper."

"Thanks," Zira miffed, then continued to stare out into the field. Woody joined their gaze.

"Say, what are ya'll lookin' at? Ain't nothin' out there."

"None of your business," Tongai said.

Woody's feathers ruffled slightly, but it did not choke his conversation filter. "I thought we's all in this together? Like a team."

"Yeah, but you're on the *other* team," Zira grunted. "Not ours."

The three birds sat quietly for a moment, two of them hoping the third would leave, but Woody was too affable to let silence break his friendships apart. Instead, he thought he would re-ignite the conversation with a light joke. "Ya know, you two have been lookin' awfully plump lately. You find some sort of all-you-can-eat buffet out here in the grassland?"

Both Tongai and Zira took immediate offense to the comment and turned to hiss at Woody. "How dare you call us fat!"

Woody's neck recoiled and his head dipped low. "Jeez, I was only teasin' . . . "

Just then, a zebra strolled into view and started munching on a leafy bush. Zira and Tongai instinctually hunkered their necks and started licking their beaks while Woody looked back and forth between the two. It was as if they had forgotten he was there.

"Why're you two gawkin' at a live zebra? Is there a lion around or somethin'?"

"Sh," Tongai hissed. "Don't scare it off."

Within moments, there was a snappy *click!* followed by an enormous blast. Woody squalled as he fluttered backwards into the grass while Tongai and Zira bounced their heads up and down in utter delight. The two laughed and laughed as Woody awkwardly rolled back onto his feet. "What 'n tarnation was that!" he cried as he fluttered back to the fence.

Instead of answering right away, Tongai and Zira looked at each other behind Woody's back. Tongai beaked, "Follow my lead," then winked at her. She nodded in delight.

"*That*, my friend, is the easiest meal you will ever get!"

Chunks had spread all over but the bulk of the carcass

laid directly in front of the trio about twenty meters out. Woody's beak started watering. "You mean, that's all for *us*?"

"Yep," Zira confirmed, stretching her wing out to point at the prize *and* to shroud the red warning sign to her right. "All you gotta do is run out there and dig in!"

"And nothin'll happen to us?"

"Of course not!" Tongai grinned. "But since we're all on the same team, you should have the first peck."

"Well hoo-wee!" Woody screeched as he hopped down from the fence. Without a moment wasted, he scuttled a beeline to the juicy half-zebra waiting out in the field. Tongai and Zira grimaced in delight with every waddled skip, step, and hop he made. They were so close to being rid of the only other vulture that knew of their secret haven they could taste it. Except . . . nothing happened. No clicks, no bangs, just the ridiculous sight of a large bird hobbling on foot with outstretched wings.

When Woody arrived at the carcass, he waved back at his friends before plunging his bald face into the warm ribcage. Zira and Tongai looked at each other with beaks hung open.

"How did he..?" Tongai asked.

"I don't know," Zira replied, then looked down at her enlarged, rumbling stomach, "but I'm getting hungry now."

Tongai nodded and started flapping his wings. He hovered for a moment and landed back on the post next to Zira. "You know, flying takes up quite a bit of energy," he said with labored breaths. "Maybe we should walk, too."

Zira nodded and they both dropped down from the fence. The two of them ambled slowly, taking great care to use the exact same path Woody had taken. About midway Tongai glanced down and noticed he could barely see his own claws anymore. He looked over at Zira, who was the same startling shape as him, and started cackling.

"What are *you* laughing at?" she hissed.

"Nothing," Tongai snickered. "Except at how fat you are!"

"Me? You're as round as a hippo!"

"Am not!"

The two vultures again squabbled back and forth until one had finally had enough. Zira shoved Tongai to the ground, causing him to roll forward on the path like a lopsided ball. After two full revolutions he ended up on his back, claws to the sky, floundering as Zira laughed herself to tears. "Help me up!" he begged, but as soon as she hopped over to say, "I told you so," they heard a snappy *click!*

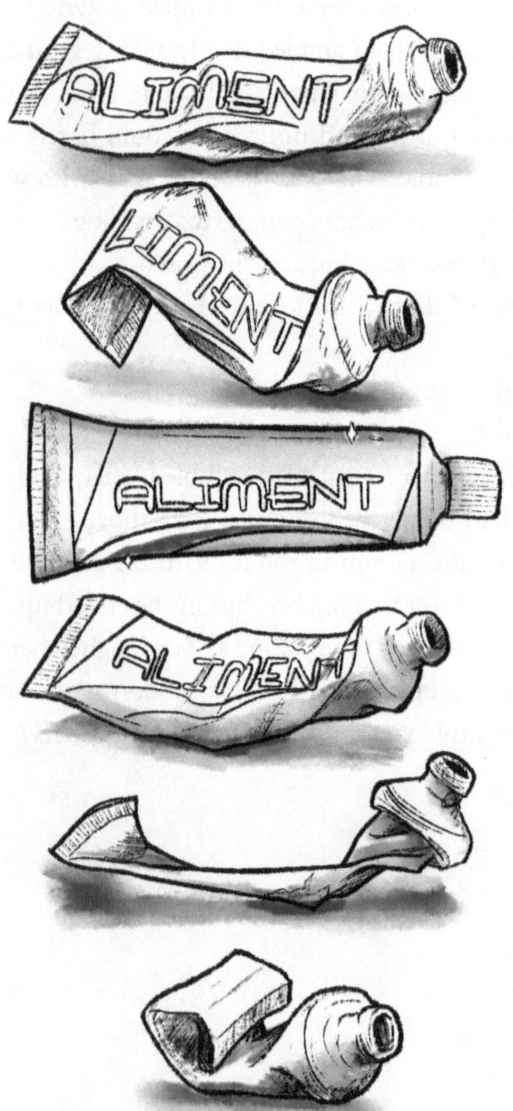
ALIMENT
LIMENT
ALIMENT
ALIMENT

POMONA

```
Tsula Nelowie - Mechanic
UEG Mission Log: Day 1
Harvest Vessel: Ceres 15
Total Crew: 6
```

> Is it recording?

> Just say whatever I want?

> Okay.

> Hi! I'm Tsula Nelowie and that was Captain James helping me with the camera. Say, "Hi," cap!

> No?

> Alrighty then.

> Let's see, where to begin . . .

> Ooh! First, check this out. You see that out the window? That's Pomona! I've only been awake for an hour and all I want to do is worship her. Who knew there could be so much green? I wonder if—

> What's that? You want me to stay on task and talk about the mission? But you said...

> Fine.

> I'll start over.

> My name is Tsula Nelowie and I'm the mechanic aboard the Ceres 15. We've been in cryosleep for fifteen years and were just re-animated about one Earth-hour ago. I say Earth-hour because soon we'll be switching over to Pomona's clock for the rest of our lives.

> Oh, hold on. Captain's gone now. Let me prop the camera up by the window so you can at least look at her while I babble on.

> One sec...

> There.

> Now where was I? Oh, right. The mission. It's hard to believe fifteen years have gone by since we left Earth for good. I was thirty at the time so I wonder if that still makes me thirty now? Who knows. I'm no astrophysicist, just the resident mechanical genius.

> On that note, it still baffles me that I got selected for this mission in the first place. I had freshly graduated UEG's Inertia Academy—with flying colors I might add—when I submitted my application as a dare from my friends. Within

a month they called to welcome me aboard the Ceres 15 on its third mission! I mean, how do you say no to that? But don't worry, these ships were designed by Sahara engineers far above my mental capacity—and even farther above my pay scale—to make sure that an actual human would be the last thing needed in case of an . . . event. So that pretty much makes me and Mendez a couple of glorified stowaways. Don't tell him that, though. To say he takes his job seriously would be an understatement.

> So what is the mission? It's not like everyone on Earth doesn't already know, but the Captain and our creepy communications guy, Tim Glanton, told me that talking through tasks and feelings is beneficial for my mental health and whatnot. Also, it's required.

< Sighs >

> Since there's more land than water on Earth—like, a lot more—it can't sustain enough food to feed its ten billion people. The solution? Start growing our crops on a planet fifteen Earth-years away. That'd be Pomona; a literal garden planet. Each of the Ceres ships harvests enough food from Pomona to feed the people back home for one whole year. Fifteen-year trips, fifteen ships...you get the idea.

> The catch? All of the harvest gets ground up into this nasty nutrient paste called Aliment; another Sahara invention. If each human sucks down one tube of Aliment per day, they'll meet the exact caloric and nutritious requirement to live a comfortable life. It's not ideal, but it's all we've got.

> You see, our colossal ship triples as interplanetary transportation, a hovering combine, and a seemingly endless storage slash processing slash product placement bin. Hell, you can probably *still* see the Sahara logo from Earth.

> Once the C-15 lands, it separates the living quarters, along with us, near the main outpost where we'll be working. Then it drops the kilometer-long combine to begin harvesting in field A-1. After five days of threshing, the storage unit is filled to the brim and the Ceres reassembles itself to begin mashing food on its fifteen-year journey back to Earth.

> Without us.

> That's right. The number one perk to being on this mission is that we get to live on beautiful Pomona! As an ongoing attempt at populating this new world, the crew from each Ceres mission gets to stay behind at a nearby campus called Colony. Once the Ceres takes off and our work is done, we'll be able to head there and eat as many fruits and vegetables as our stomachs can handle. No more drought. No more hunger. No more Aliment.

> I'm so excited to meet the people here. What have they learned? What can they cook? What do they do for fun? I can't even imagine—

> What's that?

> We're preparing for descent?

> I'll be right there.

> Welp, you heard the captain. I'm about to start the first day of the rest of my life.

> This is Veronica James, Captain, recording my mandatory daily brief. It's day two of our reanimation from stasis, and day one on Pomona's surface. Currently it's twenty-nine-hundred Pomona time and we are aboard the United Earth Government's Ceres 15 vessel, third expedition. My crew is in good health and morale is steady.

> Nelowie, Mendez, Glanton, Lewis, Bloom, and myself made full recoveries from our fifteen-year cryosleep and are in top physical and mental condition. My first order as captain was to have them log their daily briefs while they were fresh, then assume their stations while the C-15 landed safely.

> Early this morning, about three-hundred Pomona time, we touched down at the designated LZ without a single hitch and the C-15 disassembled itself immediately and routinely. The crew also began their duties in tandem. The weather is pleasant, the crops are bountiful, and even I stole a few moments during my appointed lunch break to appreciate the objective beauty of this planet.

> Reminds me of my childhood on Earth.

<...>

> Apologies for getting off-track.

> Since in yesterday's log I chose to reflect on my personal condition and observations, today I am opting to report on the crew. Three outstanding graduates of the UEG Inertia Academy and three appointees from Sahara Industries. I will begin with Aquiles Mendez and proceed in alphabetical order by first name.

> Aquiles Mendez is the C-15's operations manager. He is both a software and mechanical engineer and highly decorated in each field. Much of the Ceres' routines are automated, so his primary directives are co-piloting the ship, monitoring the harvesters, and keeping an eye out for bugs in the irrigation software. Mendez works from sunup to sundown, which is approximately six hours longer on Pomona than on Earth, and is as efficient as any machine. His ebullient optimism is welcome among myself and the crew.

> Kendrick Lewis is our Sahara-issued security official, though I'm not convinced his position is essential to the mission. It is of my opinion that when on a harvest vessel manned by scientists and engineers there is very little emotional conflict. However, both the UEG and Sahara require their crews to learn basic self-defense and combat-submission before launch, so he had been of value on Earth. But now that we're here his day-to-day consists of walking the halls, monitoring security cameras, and occasionally interrupting the crew when they least need interrupting.

> Side note on Lewis: I don't know if there is history between

the two, but if he doesn't learn to squelch his advances on Bloom until Colony, I may be compelled to use some of his training against him.

> Speaking of, Scarlett Bloom is the resident horticulturist. I'm not one to assume another's general attractiveness, but the crew has struggled to keep their eyes off of her, Lewis being the most concerning. It didn't help that none of us had even met Bloom until takeoff, but Sahara insists that her research is paramount to the health of future harvests. I, admittedly, am not as studied in plant biology, but I can at the very least grasp that we're on an alien planet sowing alien crops into alien soil. Thankfully, Bloom is a professional and has already collected the samples she needs before retiring to her lab. I do not expect to see her much between now and relocation day.

> Tim Glanton is another corporate-appointee and is in charge of communications. Since Pomona is too far away from Earth to transmit live data, he collects and compresses it, our recordings included, and prepares it for Uplink—an experimental "piggybacking" of data transfer technology using a combination of Ceres 1 through 14 and various Sahara satellites. Uplink is still young, but it's Glanton's job to figure it out. As for the person himself, he predominantly carries around a salty demeanor. General trust in authority is not his strong suit so I constantly have to remind him that I can place him back in stasis. At least he stays out of the rest of the crew's way for the most part.

> And finally, Tsula Nelowie. Our bright and young mechanic. I'm afraid that she may be more head-in-the-stars and less feet-on-the-ground with this mission. She and I are both aware of how many systems on the C-15 are automated so that leaves her with little to do when operations run accordingly. This . . . free time . . . leads her to explore other interests. Mendez doesn't tolerate it, she generally avoids Lewis and Glanton due to their crassness, which leaves myself and Bloom for her to bother. Once the C-15 leaves, I believe Tsula will thrive on Pomona. For now, let's just hope a screw comes loose for her to fix.

> Alright then.

> This has been Veronica James, Captain, concluding my mandatory mission brief. It's day two of our reanimation from stasis, and day one on Pomona's surface. Currently it's twenty-nine-hundred-and-thirty-four Pomona time and we are aboard the United Earth Government's Ceres 15 vessel, third expedition. My crew is in good health and morale is steady.

> Oh, sorry. Excuse me.

> How long has my nose been bleeding?

> My apologies.

> I'll be sure to log this in the medical briefing immediately following.

> Over.

—

> Greetings, Earthlings.

<Heh>

> I've always wanted to say that.

> This is Aquiles Mendez. Operations manager aboard the Ceres 15. It's day two of the harvest and things couldn't be looking better. I get to monitor the inputs of that hovering, kilometer-long combine and then track the outputs as produce is separated from plant. It's thrilling to witness this evolution of a machine that was once only suited to separate grain from chaff. Now it will accept anything thrown at it.

> Now if only Sahara hadn't automated it so I could drive it myself.

> Yesterday, day one on Pomona's surface, fields A1 through B7 were successfully harvested. Things I hadn't seen since childhood are growing more abundantly and massively than I could ever have imagined. Pumpkins the size of houses, strawberries the circumference of cars, and cucumbers as long as boats with spinach leaves as wide as sails, all of them collected without waste and sent into the colossal processing bin for Aliment production.

> Aliment, what a miracle invention. Sahara may be the

only standing corporation left on Earth, but we should all be thanking them. It was Sahara who discovered Pomona. Sahara who designed and built the Ceres fleet. And Sahara who combined the outputs of a hundred and twenty different crops and condensed them into a single tube of nutrient-rich paste that keeps humanity thriving.

> And that's not to mention the beautiful efficiency of it all. How much more we've been able to accomplish since Aliment. It almost makes me sad that we'll devolve to preparing our own food once we take residency here on Pomona. Such time wasted! Fortunately, we've gained six working hours by default.

> Argh!

> There it is again. The throbbing behind my right eye. It's been extremely persistent.

> A side effect of stasis, I'm sure.

> I will continue to record my instances until the medical team at Colony can look into it.

> Three more days.

> Headache aside, I often wonder what Colony life is like. I presume they'll have a position for me to continue monitoring these irrigation systems. Such excitement, to watch the new crops replace the old. To record their growth and discover new efficiencies. Bloom will certainly become a vital resource as I continue to learn about Pomonan agriculture.

> What?

> No, Tsula, I can't entertain you right now.

> Because I have to finish my daily brief and then I'm back to monitoring coolant levels at the processing bin.

> Goodbye.

> That girl. Her energy level seems higher now than when I met her sixteen years ago. Another byproduct of being in cryosleep for fifteen, surely. I will report her intrusion along with my headache.

> The combine just completed field D14 and is on to F. I love watching the proficiency of this process. Instead of making an unnecessary three-point turn, the hovering capabilities allow it to shift over to an adjacent field without disturbing the land. The power thrumming through that great machine . . .

> Perhaps in a past life I could have been a farmer.


```
Tim Glanton - Communications
UEG Mission Log: Day 4
Harvest Vessel: Ceres 15
Total Crew: 5
```


> Figures.

> We already lost one.

> Late last night that young girl—Tsula was her name?—decided to strip naked and walk off into one of the fields. All we could find of her was her clothes. Now everyone's up in

arms askin' me to keep searchin' for her. Ain't that Lewis's job?

> Not like I don't have enough to worry about as it is, tryin' to hammer out Uplink. I think Sahara made it this complex on purpose. Like, you're tellin' me we can send fifteen space-combines to a planet fifteen years away to harvest a year's worth of shit paste for the folks back home, but we can't send a damn video log?

> Not to mention we haven't even heard from Colony.

> Look, I've studied communications my whole life. I know how easy it is to transmit radio signals from one ship to another. At the absolute MINIMUM we should be able to chat with folks on the same damn planet.

> Yet here we sit. Dead silence.

> Somethin's up.

< . . . >

> Hell, I might as well get it all out before I wind up like the girl.

> Don't ask me how I came by this, but I've heard that the UEG and Sahara are neck-deep in some sort of android program. You know, dark, strictly off-the-books shit. That they're only sending humans to Pomona for planetary morale. Makes all the sheep back home feel warm and fuzzy to think we're out here pioneering the future.

> Well I got news for 'em: the future ain't us.

> I mean, think about it. Why the hell would Sahara bother freezing us meatbags when they designed the C-15 to

completely automate itself? All I do is sit around and scratch my ass. Sounds like Tsula was doin' the same.

> Or...

> Maybe Tsuala WAS an android. Maybe she just malfunctioned and her body told her to go thataway.

> Nah. Girl seemed to have issues after being thawed out. Too uppity to be made of metal.

> I bet it's Mendez. All day every day he crunches numbers without sleep. Crunches numbers for what, though? The ship tracks it all for him. Unless he's literally plugged into the system...

> Or what about that Scarlett? With a body like that she had to be designed in a lab.

<Heh>

> Lewis I figure is alright. Sahara-issued guard should be a red flag, but he stops in to show me security footage of Scarlett bending over to pick things up. Behavior that creepy can only be associated with humans.

> Could be the captain. What better use of a robot than to keep us lowly humans in line? In fact, it's almost definitely her. She constantly makes us record our every thought on these videos like we're little lab rats.

> I'm definitely gonna keep my eye on her.

< . . . >

> Whoever's watching this is probably wondering why I even signed up for Pomona.

> Easy answer.

> Aliment.
> I don't trust food that's auto-processed inside a big space machine and then fed to us in tubes. Can you think of an easier way for UEG to pump tracking chips into our bodies?
> Glanton, out.


```
Kendrick Lewis - Security
UEG Mission Log: Day 5
Harvest Vessel: Ceres 15
Total Crew: 2
```


> This is EXACTLY why you need security detail on a manned space mission.
> Last night, I woke up to Aquiles Mendez walking straight into the goddamn combine. His body had been turned to pulp and sprayed out with the berries before I could even get my shoes on. Dumb bastard.
> And if THAT ain't enough paperwork, today I walked in on Glanton and Captain James at each other's throats in the mess hall. Glanton was accusing the captain of being a robot or some shit and James was telling him she'd put him back in cryo. Her nose was bleeding to beat all hell. I thought Glanton had hit her so I barked at him to stand down . . .
> Jesus.
> Veronica turned to face me, Glanton rammed a dinner

knife into her neck, then she turned back and did the same.

< . . . >

> By the time I reached them, they had both dropped to the ground. I yanked the silverware out and filled their wounds with BioSeal. They were shaking real bad. Once they went unconscious I dragged their dead weight back into the cryopods and put them on ice.

> Lord knows if they'll make it.

< . . . >

> Shit.

> Since I'm here, I'm just gonna say it.

> Everyone's been feeling weird since landing on this damn planet. Hysteria, headaches, nosebleeds, irritability, delusions. At first I chalked it up to the increased gravity, but the Ceres 15 was designed to mimic Pomona's rotation so our bodies would already be acclimated. Then I got to thinking it was the Aliment. But we've been eating that for decades on Earth without losing our damn minds.

> I can't say what for sure, but something got to those people.

> Something.

> Something in the air.

> Now it's just me and Scarlett. My girl. My North Star.

> I meant to check on her sooner, but it takes a while to scrub someone else's blood off your hands.

> On the bright side, she's seemed to have kept it together as tightly as I have. We both have a mental toughness that makes us such a good match. Some could say we were made

for each other.
> Despite all of this tragedy, I look forward to our life together at Colony.


```
Scarlett Bloom - Horticulturist
UEG Mission Log: Return
Harvest Vessel: Ceres 15
Total Crew: 1
```


> This is UEG Survey-Synth, serial number PM-C-15-SB, also referred to as Scarlett Bloom, reporting successful completion of this third expedition of the harvest vessel, Ceres 15.

> Crop yield has been exceptional, producing the most raw material to date. Pomona's unusual soil and Earth's staple crops have provided the perfect catalyst for the micro fungi—dubbed Hyper Septica—to thrive. Since all three work in symbiosis to produce approximately five percent higher yields each cycle, I will continue to advise against the development of any antifungal herbicides or soil treatments.

> Compiling data from the previous two C-15 missions, and the rest collected from Ceres 1 through 14, I predict final harvest time to be reduced to four Pomona days in six Earth-years, then three Pomona days in twenty-three Earth-years.

> For this mission, recorded survivability is again determined

to be zero. The negative side effects of the soil-enriching Hyper Septica still persist from its reproductive spores. Immediate human contact with the airborne spores results in hyperactive brain activity that heightens one's deepest emotions. At this recording, the mortality rate is still effectively one hundred percent, though this experimentation may have produced one variable.

> Tsula.

> Following are the results from Case 45, or, formal name, The Joint Pomona Study On Human Biology and Its Reactions to Hyper Septica.

< . . . >

> Aquiles Mendez.

> Mendez suffered from throbbing headaches directly behind the right eye which quickly shifted his admiration of complex machines to obsession. He perished on day four.

< . . . >

> Tim Glanton.

> Both Glanton and Captain James reported nosebleeds and irritability throughout their time on Pomona. They took each other's lives on day five. Lewis placed their bodies in cryo-pods, but I have since removed and disposed of them.

< . . . >

> Veronica James.

> See above.

< . . . >

> Kendrick Lewis.

> Lewis became delusional on day one. His obsession with the female body I inhabit altered his judgment and I was all he could focus on. Though he survived through day five, I was forced to terminate him after he broke into my lab with a crowbar and threatened to take both of our lives out of, quote, love.

< . . . >

> Tsula Nelowie.

> Tsula is a peculiar case because she is our first subject without a confirmed death. From what I can observe, she underwent a minor bout of hysteria—exiting unclothed into field E17—but she never appeared to be life-threatening. If I were to speculate, exposure to Hyper Septica merely enhanced her curiosity and affinity for nature.

< . . . >

> I will send a recommendation through encrypted Uplink for UEG Survey-Synth PM-C-1-AM to search for Nelowie's body and recover samples. If her blood yields promising results, perhaps Sahara can synthesize a vaccine in another century or so.

> Optimistically, Colony could then begin its transition from fiction to reality.

> To conclude, Ceres 15 has now returned to orbit and is finalizing launch routines. System checks are in order and Aliment conversion is taking place.

> Expected return to Earth: Fourteen years and three hundred days.

CIRC**Ł**E

In the blistering heat of Botswana, a torrential thunderhead bloomed in the background. Great palms creaked slowly beneath the billowing clouds—digging deeper, deeper their roots—and beneath their hardened trunks thick Cogangrass whispered warnings to the anxious wind. *Another has entered the jungle*, they said, but soon that muggy atmosphere could no longer sustain itself and fat raindrops began drowning out the signal. One, two, three, pitter-patters on a canvas tent below; foreboding knocks of what was yet to come.

"We need to leave now!" the tracker barked over a clap of encroaching thunder. "Pack what you can and load the trucks!"

Within the camp of three tents, two gutted Land Rovers, and one hissing fire pit, men skittered around like flies on a nearly-picked carcass, snatching up what remained before being shooed away by something greater. Every man was in a frenzy. Every man but one.

"We can't abandon the trail! We might lose it!"

The tracker stopped and turned, hauling a heavy case that slumped his shoulders. His boots now left soft impressions in the saturating dirt. "If we do not flee from this camp, we may not survive the night. We can try again in the dry season."

Opposing the tracker was a tall man dressed in olive and khaki fatigues and a matching wide-brimmed hat. A hunter. His boots too made squishy patterns as he confronted the concerned tracker. "You must be joking! I've given everything to be here and I must see it through to the end!"

The tracker glanced skyward. The sun had abandoned them for a caustic, jade horizon hungry enough to swallow them whole. He then looked around at his men filing like ants from the tents to the trucks. They were all losing to the mud. Back to the hunter he said, "We go. Now."

"I cannot," concluded the hunter. "A delicate shape is at stake."

Thunder cracked again, this time directly overhead, and the shock of it knocked one of the tracker's men to the ground. The others dropped their trunks and slid over to lift their fallen companion, but the rain was now so relentless that their boots could find no traction, ensuing a skirmish of mud and men.

"No," the tracker declared. "We are leaving."

Displeased with the resistance being met, the hunter lunged for the heavy gun case in the tracker's arms and tried to pry it away. However, instead of fighting back, the tracker simply released his grip on the object and watched the stubborn hunter slip in the gunk and fall with a splat. "Suit yourself."

The men were now out of the mess and packed into the Land Rovers. The lead truck pulled up to the tracker with headlamps and fog lamps and roof lamps ablaze, piercing beams for the long night to follow. On the ground, water had already filled the fresh tire tracks and the sense of urgency between the men swelled. The tracker climbed into the back, leaving behind boot prints that soon morphed to small ponds.

"It is already tagged," the tracker called out to the hunter as the trucks churned slowly through the soup. "Just remember: When you kill a king, you are at the mercy of his kingdom."

Nothing else could be heard following. The monsoon howled at full capacity and the hunter stood livid beneath it. Clutching the heavy case, he trudged back to the last standing tent and went inside. The ground was a swamp and water had claimed everything on its level. Two elevated cots were all that remained. He laid the large case in one and took sleep in the other, relying on grit and duty equally to protect him through the night.

———

The following morning the hunter awoke to the singeing heat of canvas on skin as much of the tent had collapsed during the storm. He pushed the hot fabric away and stumbled out of what remained of the zippered entry. The ground of the encampment still resembled a thick paste, but the tracks left behind by tires and boots had drained and made themselves known again in the light.

Light!

The hunter looked upwards and felt the uncompromising power of an African sun on his unprotected skin and began rolling down the damp sleeves of his fatigues. While he dried he took stock of what supplies had not washed away. There was a waterlogged backpack, a sealed trunk of food rations, some necks of canteens poking out from the hardening mud, and little else. He collected and laid what he could out to dry and returned to the tent.

Inside he snapped open the clasps of the heavy plastic case and sighed relief at the site of his dry weapons; heirlooms priceless to him and him alone. He lifted out his childhood rifle and inspected the stock, the barrel, the hammer, then glanced down the scope. All was in precise order. Next he reached for his sidearm and went through the same motions before clipping it into a holster already around his waist. Finally, he picked up a large, engraved Bowie knife asleep in a bespoke sheathe and slid it onto his belt. A family phrase regarding that the knife only be used as a last resort popped into his consciousness so he squeezed the handle respectfully before releasing.

Outside the gear was now dry enough to stow. The hunter checked a gold compass clipped to the side of the backpack and looked in the direction of northwest. That was the heading the tracker had used in the days prior, and it was the heading he would continue to use today. Gear and weapons secured to his body, the hunter stepped widely over a deep tire track left behind like a crinkled snakeskin and resumed the hunt alone.

Around noon, or when the sun was highest, the ground began to ripple. Whether it be cicadas, the last of the evaporating storm, or his own skin burning, an eternal sizzle followed his ears about. It was hot. Too hot for any man to wander about unshaded, but the hunter pressed on with nothing except resolve to simmer his blood.

The metal compass was not consulted again until it was cool enough to be touched, which incidentally was just before nightfall. All day the hunter had walked due north without so much as an inkling of west. *Drat!* he thought, then kicked the dirt. It was as dry and clay-like as before the storm, and told no stories of tracks—human or otherwise. A long pull from his third emptied canteen brought him down to just one and he wiped his forehead with a sweat-stained sleeve while cursing at the direction he missed.

An even lower sun now painted the safari as red as blood. A nearby thicket of tall grass and a few palms offered the only suitable camp for the night. The hunter entered the patch and stomped out a flat circle in the grass just his size. He laid down using his backpack as a pillow, crossed his fingers behind his head, and watched intently as the night devoured the day.

High above, stars twinkled unhindered by human light, each as bright as Earth's own sun. There were too many to count and the hunter wondered if any housed thriving worlds of their own. If any shared the same responsibilities. But it was not long until the inky hues of jet, navy, and violet challenged the limits of his focus and a weight fell over his eyes. Then a dream came to him. A memory.

Look, son, a voice instructed from the ether. A fragment inside the hunter's sleeping mind observed the stardusted outline of a fallen stag. A meteor had pierced its breast, but its cosmic lungs still rose and fell. *Your first kill. Man has unintentionally, and sometimes intentionally, disrupted the natural order of this world. Some populations now grow in excess while other ones dwindle, causing the circle of life to distort and become unbalanced. For a circle to have strength we must understand that our duty as hunters, as sportsmen, as human beings, is to repair and preserve this delicate shape.*

CIRCLE

Now, use my knife to complete this circle . . .

Indeed sleep had taken interest in the hunter, but so had others. Nocturnal eyes from all around the sub-Sahara watched him in his slumber, heeding the monsoon's warning of another, curious about the outcome. They began calling out their words using a symphony of howls and caws and whoops and grunts. Unbeknownst to those who do not speak the languages of the jungle, a message was being delivered as swiftly as the rising sun.

———

Midway through the next afternoon the hunter emptied the last drop of water from his final canteen. He cursed out loud, for there were no ears he knew of that could understand him, then swallowed dryly before sauntering on, duty demanding he see this through.

However, the heat persisted and signs of wildlife remained elusive. The sky was silver-hot like reflective foil. There were no holes for water nor trees for shade. Even the breeze refused a breath of relief. The hunter's tongue scraped against the roof of his mouth in the same way his boots dragged across the soil. His legs were strained from the day's eternal walk and it would not be long before surrounding forces would overcome him.

Another hour passed and the sun once again bled the horizon in a deep scarlet. The hunter dropped to his knees. Exhausted, panting, bordering delusion, he scanned desperately for one more night's shelter. A grove of thick Baobabs and bushes beckoned him, but from far too far in the east. Before and behind nothing but arid dirt and gossiping patches of Cogangrass sat thirsty for his collapse. To the west, however, was a fortuitous cluster of large boulders; massive at the center and marginally smaller on the flanks. Atop the center stone sat a short, crooked Acacia tree still green from the recent rain. To the hunter and his fatigued mind, the odd formation resembled that of a throne with an umbrella for shade.

He gathered what was left of his strength and his wits and rose to his feet and lumbered towards the large rocks outlined by the crimson of a setting sun. Heat and sweat tugged at his fatigue and his fatigues, but rest was only meters away. This would not be his final night. He would fashion little water traps to collect the morning dew, recharge by way of heavy sleep, then search for a body of water in the coolness of dawn.

But the hunter's scheming was interrupted when a shadowed figure climbed on the farthest stone to the left. He paused and watched as it sat upright and still as the evening air. Then he braved another step. A similar silhouette climbed onto the stone at the right's edge. It too sat as frozen and regal as the opposing figure.

The hunter's eyes narrowed, but it was hard to hold focus. If he did not rest his body and mind soon he would become an indulgence for hyenas and then later vultures. He needed time, but time seemed to fill the vacant stones with identical figures until only one remained: the center.

"Do not take another step!" thundered a voice from behind the formation.

The sudden command formed an intangible wall that stopped the hunter dead in his tracks. He froze. Just then, an enormous shadow rose from behind the center stone and perched on its crest, just beneath the umbrella-esque Acacia. Heavy growls saturated the air.

Vision skewed from the westward red sun, the hunter raised a palm to shield his brow. "Is that you, tracker? I told you I must see this through to the end."

"The end of what, human?" goaded the one now lunging down from the center stone. It landed roughly a meter away from the hunter and began plodding a slow, clockwise circle in the tall grass. "Your days?"

The hunter, adrenaline restoring his cognition, could now see that the figure was no tracker at all. Instead it walked on four powerful legs, had a prodigious golden mane, and clasped to its left ear was a lime-green tag.

"I've come without malice," stated the hunter, reaching carefully around back for his prized rifle.

Noticing this, the male lion leapt like a great grasshopper and swiped the weapon away with a mighty paw. The rifle landed in the deep grass some distance away, broken beyond future use. A piece of the hunter may have broken along with it.

"All your kind knows is malice," the lion said, continuing its circle in the grass around the human.

The hunter pivoted, keeping the immediate threat to his face. "While I am here to take one life, yes, it is only to repair the circle of others'."

The lion shook its head as if wicking water and snorted a beastly laugh. "The circle of life? Is that a maxim sung to human children so they feel warm about the terror they will inevitably cause?"

A chuffing rabble echoed from the tops of the nearby stone formation, stealing the hunter's attention for a moment. An entire pride of lionesses sat tittering at him.

"And just how do you plan to see your action through?" the great lion taunted, demanding once again the hunter's attention. "Your muscles are soft, your flesh is fragile, your teeth are flat. Without your stick of metal you are but a toy to me."

The hunter kept facing the male, who had completed a full circle, and hoped the large cat's propensity to chat would serve a suitable distraction as he reached for his sidearm. Slowly. "It is my kind's duty to repair and preserve the delicate circle."

"Preserve?" boomed the lion with venomous disgust. "*Your* kind consumes *our* lands, harvests *our* food, kidnaps *our* cubs, sells *our* bones. You only stand here with an unquenchable thirst for pride."

The hunter studied the lion as it circled. Its vast paws pressed lengths of stiff Cogangrass into the earth, forming a natural trail in its wake. Its mane feathered to and fro with the rise and fall of its sinewy shoulders. Its stride stretched and contracted the powerful plexus of muscles throughout the back and haunches. A considerable sacrifice.

But the hunter needed more time to position himself. "And what of your pride?"

Somehow these words hindered the great lion. It paused in the circle made around its prey to exchange eyes with its pride. This was enough for the hunter to unclip the leather band holding his sidearm in place and remove it from the holster.

But a lion's sense of hearing is only seconded by its reflexes. Before the hunter's act of deception could bear any fruit, the lion's ear flicked and its head had whipped back to face the man. Another swift leap and a swipe of the paw and this weapon too was lost to the brush.

"Coward!" seethed the lion, returning to its circular stroll. "To use my pride against me..."

Still, the hunter had one last trick up his sleeve. It was in the shape of a large Bowie knife that had once belonged to his father. The one he had learned to respectfully kill and clean his game with. The one that would have to be drawn at exactly the right moment...

"Why do you think that tag is clipped to your ear?" the hunter asked.

The lion flicked its head as if it had just been reminded of something it had worked hard to forget. "Another act of human destruction, no less."

"Not quite," the hunter responded matter-of-factly. "You've been selected."

A low growl emphasized the large cat's natural curiosity. "Indulge me."

"We've been watching you closely," divulged the hunter, "for a long time. Your presence has served well for tourism, but your prime reproductive years have passed. No cubs have graced your pride in nearly a decade yet you continue to ward off younger, more fertile males with life-ending violence."

The lionesses seemed to have heard the hunter's sentiment due to some guttural sounds made between them, but the lion paid them no mind. "And this is of any concern to you, why?"

"I do not align with the humans who have damaged the delicate circle with their greed and their pollution and their superstitions, but I can repair it. Removing you from this pride will allow it to grow. Allow it to thrive."

All fell quiet in the setting sky. The lion looked down at its paws and the circle it had created around the hunter, seemed to consider the human's words. Then it looked back to its pride with wise but weary eyes. All the lionesses were exchanging looks and rumbles back and forth between one another. Questioning. They agreed it had been many moons since they had nursed cubs. But was this the human's fault?

Or their own male's?

While the lionesses held their male's attention, the hunter reached for his father's knife. He felt the worn handle and thought of his journey. The lessons he learned. The virtues he held. The species he had saved by fulfilling these dark tasks. He shifted his foot for balance, sliding it across the arid ground, counting on the flick of his opponent's tagged ear.

Enraged, the lion lunged.

The hunter drew.

And the sun set once again on the kingdom.

THE GRAND HOTEL

As the car veered onto the dusty byway, bits of gravel clinked against its mangled chassis. Old, balding tires slipped and grabbed, slipped and grabbed, slipped and grabbed as they crunched against the loose rock. The driver obstinately lurched the engine forward while tender memories of music and laughter faded with each turning mile on the speedometer. At this point the car was essentially a contorted hunk of metal on rails, but after all that time spent parked outside of offices run by men whose only jobs were to give sentences or collect fees, there was never any funds for repairs. *Had it been a year already?* It didn't matter. The only destination this bucket of bolts needed to reach was at the end of this road.

When gravel turned into barren field, the sedan creaked to a halt in front of a lonely, decrepit structure. Out stepped a man without so much as a suitcase or a hat. *Surely this can't be it?* The man slammed the wretched door shut and it ricocheted back without latching, as if the car itself was begging him to get back inside. He might have even listened, too, if it hadn't been repeating that same gesture day after day for nearly a full lap around the sun. No, the man had a reservation to make, so he left the door to sway in the wind.

From a distance the hotel delivered promise in the greying sunlight. The Victorian structure looked to be no more than five stories tall with a slightly raised tower at all four corners and a bowed entryway; possibly to encase a mezzanine or elaborate staircase. But up close one could say it had been abandoned of all life centuries ago. As the man inched closer he quickly noticed missing bricks along the foundation, paint curling away from the siding, rotted sills around arched windows, loose shingles lifting with each gust, and a massive double-door entry that he believed would dissolve to mulch if he knocked too vigorously. He stole a glance back towards his crumpled burden, dripping oil and spitting steam, when an icy breeze inched up his spine to remind him why he came all the way out to the middle of nowhere in the first place.

At the double-doors the man jiggled their rusted handles,

but they wouldn't budge. *Strange, I was told this place never closed.* He gave them another tug when a cluster of cobwebs midway up caught his attention. Something lustrous veiled behind them. He used the arm of his jacket to swipe away the vacated webs and revealed a peculiar object. A once-brass hand was clutching a ring made up of two intertwined snakes as it would a lantern. It was almost as if the holder was discarding some poisonous rope.

First the man studied the uniquely forged knocker for fear it would bring harm to his bare hand if he touched it. Then he remembered that day was descending quickly and was taking the temperature along with it. With eyes closed, he outstretched his arm and gripped the viperous ring. To his relief it didn't bite. He slammed it against a metal plate fastened to the door once, twice, three times, and stepped back for an answer. There were no footsteps to be heard. He checked the horizon just as the sun shared its last wink before turning in for the night. Belief he had made a foolhardy mistake started churning his stomach when a clicking noise startled him. The door had unlatched, silently inching itself inward to reveal a narrow, dark crevice.

A few moments passed until it was clear to the man that no one was on the other side to receive him. He blew some warm air into his cupped hands and decided to push the door open and slip in. Immediately he was greeted by a vast, unlit lobby with chairs arranged around circular tables which were, in turn, arranged around an oxidized fountain.

Atop the fountain kneeled a thinly robed woman whose head was tilted up towards the ceiling. She appeared to be crying; or at least she had been before the water dried ages ago. After he took a few creaky steps towards an antique lamp, he noticed the entire room was already blanketed in dusty moonbeams. *Odd*, he thought, considering the sun had only just gone down.

"Good evening, Mr. Jones," a voice hailed in the void, nearly ceasing the man's heart. He stumbled backwards from the lamp in frantic search of its origin. Opposite the moonlit entryway was a desk below a wide mezzanine; now illuminated with soft candle light. Behind the desk was a bellhop, almost skeletal, as if an animate extension of the exposed studs and joists of the archaic architecture itself. The bellhop wore a smile, a suit, and a cylindrical hat that, if the man could study long enough without being considered rude, didn't fully rest on top of his head. But instead of concerning himself further, the man chalked the optics up to poor lighting and approached the desk.

"Welcome to The Grand Hotel," the bellhop spoke through a wide, desolate smile. "You are just in time."

The man couldn't find himself to say anything. The very idea of this place sounded so asinine that he was too embarrassed to bring it up.

The unwavering smile decided to interrupt the man's ineptitude. "Have you stayed with us before, Mr. Jones?"

"I, uh," the man mumbled. "No, I haven't."

"It is only in jest!" the bellhop exclaimed while folding his hands together knowingly. His smile remained firm and cold. "I have just the room for you. One night, I presume?"

The man didn't know exactly how this place operated. *Do I get more nights if I ask nicely?* "One night is fine."

"Of course it is."

For a moment, the bellhop's empty eyes looked not just *into* the man's own, but *through* them. He felt like his entire life story was being skimmed. Then, just as soon as the scan had started, the bellhop grabbed a giant nearby book and flipped it open; dust plumed in every direction. The candlelight flickered as the bellhop dragged a boney finger down an endless list of hand-scrawled names until it stopped at what the man could only assume was Jones. He watched quietly as the bellhop retrieved a feathered quill from a nearby jar of black ink and quickly scribbled something down. When the last marking was complete, the bellhop slammed the book shut and returned to the man with an already familiar, lifeless smile. "Right this way, Mr. Jones."

"How much do I owe you?"

"Your price will be paid at checkout," the bellhop replied as he walked around the front desk. "Now, follow me."

The two started up a curved stairway that looked as though they had barely survived a swarm of termites. Then they crossed the crumbling mezzanine. At the end they turned left and entered a dim hallway that illuminated itself once the bellhop had entered. *Funny, I didn't see a lightswitch.*

Rickety wooden floors lined by patchy, colorless runners led them down an endless passage. The first thing the man noticed was they had been passing room after room of closed doors with no indicating numbers or labels on them. Eventually the man's mind numbed from repetition so he tried focusing on the creaking floor beneath. *Is it just my feet making noise?* But every time the man would try to stop and listen, the bellhop broke the silence with polite quips such as, "We at The Grand Hotel value our customer's privacy," and, "We will never disturb a guest until checkout."

Some time went on and the man soon began to tune out the bellhop's chatter. Then, unexpectedly, a slightly-opened door broke the monotony and caught his attention. He paused, leaving the bellhop to continue down the hall, and silently poked his head inside the room. The faint light from the hallway illuminated a rusty wireframe bed supporting a single mattress. No other furniture occupied the small space. On top of the bed laid a woman cradling two young children. They didn't appear to be moving, but they also didn't appear to be sleeping.

Suddenly, a rigid hand captured the man's shoulder and eased him away from the door. "Like I said," the bellhop gleamed, "we value our customer's privacy."

That was warning enough for the man to continue down the incessant hallway without question. But as they carried on more and more doors were left hanging ajar. When he could, the man would secretly steal glances. In one he saw a middle-aged man clutching a greying golden retriever; in another, an elderly couple laid in a deep, loving embrace. And another—

"We have arrived."

The bellhop held the unmarked door open with his slender arm and his unceasing smile encouraged the man to enter. Inside was the same wireframe bed as all the other rooms, and nothing else.

"Would you like me to take your coat?"

The man shook his head. "That's alright."

"Very well," the bellhop bowed. "Please, make yourself comfortable."

The pleasantries seemed strangely vague and informal to the man. *Shouldn't there be some sort of ritual or something?* Nevertheless, he asked just to make sure. "Do I just lay there?"

"Whatever you wish," the bellhop averred.

After a few steps inward, the glow of faint hallway light disappeared along with the man's chauffeur, leaving behind only the hazy beams of the moon. He never heard his door latch, but he knew he was all alone. Even more alone than before. When he reached the bed he decided to leave his coat and shoes on the floor. Then he pulled the neatly tucked sheets back from the pillow and slid underneath. *If anything, I'll get a good night's rest.*

What felt like hours elapsed when the man noticed his breath condensing above his face. Although there had been no audible hum from a furnace or the hiss of a radiator, and despite all of the structural cracks allowing outside air inside, the temperature in the room hadn't changed in the slightest. *Maybe I'm just numb from traveling for so long.* His coat was still on the floor, but when he reached down to pick it up he noticed two interruptions in the line of silver moonlight at the base of the door. Then, silently, it opened.

Standing just behind the aperture was the most breathtaking silhouette the man had ever laid eyes upon. Like a masterpiece painted inside the doorframe, he traced every curve, every line, every texture of detail with his weary eyes; cross-checking them with memory. Only then did his mind confirm the unmistakable shape as genuine. She didn't move, she didn't speak, but he knew it was her.

Elated tears swelled on the man's face and he sat up hoping she remembered him, praying she had forgiven him. One foot broke the threshold. *She does remember!* The woman glided effortlessly to the bedside and he slid over to make room for her. As if they had never lost a day, she crawled in and placed a hand on his chest, inviting him to lie back down. Through his tears he smiled at her and she returned the sentiment with one of her own. Not a cold, lifeless grin like the bellhop, but a warm, effervescent smile that could soften the most callous of regrets.

While they laid together, the man softly ran his fingers across her once-wounded face. All of the cuts, all of the bruises, all of that shattered bone, now nowhere to be found.

He had so many questions. But every time he began to speak she would either slide her legs between his own, nuzzle her head into his chest, or just continue to silently share her warmth with him. *What's left to be said anyways? She knows I love her, knows it was an accident.* Finally at peace, all the man desired was to wrap her tightly in his arms and absorb each passing hour to the fullest.

Following the first beam of sunlight to squeeze through a crack in the ceiling came a gentle knock on the door. The man chose to say nothing, for nothing could ever be more important to him than her. Instead of a second knock, the door simply floated open to reveal another silhouette: the bellhop. His smile somehow reflected the single sunray as he spoke without haste. "It is time for checkout, Mr. Jones."

No! The man froze, his mind racing to find excuses. *I haven't had enough time! There is so much more I want to tell her, so much we could still do. We could take that trip to India we had always talked about. We could buy an acreage outside of the city. We could start a family . . . No. I'm not letting her go. Not again.*

"Mr. Jones, your time is up."

The man tried to sit upright, but the weight of the hand on his chest grew. She wouldn't let him move. His gaze left the bellhop's illusory smile and returned to hers. She closed her eyes and nodded at him; a motion that silently told him exactly what he needed to hear. *She's . . . she's saying it's okay. That all is forgiven. And she's right. These last few moments together are worth the price.*

"Mr. Jones, are you ready?"

The man looked once more at the only piece of himself that had ever made him whole, gripped it tight, and, knowing he would soon hold it again, replied, "I'm ready."

THE INTERNAL STRUGGLE OF JÅMISON LINÐE

On a mid-spring morning, just off the Atlantic side of Key Largo, an assembly of snorkelers reached their destination and prepared to enter the water. Among the party was Jamison Linde, who was quadruple-checking his equipment before his descent into the sun-kissed shallows.

Linde was never a man to embark on such exciting adventures, and perhaps even more so after the unfortunate circumstances of the previous year, yet here he had found himself. His routine following those dark days consisted of eight hours at work and sixteen at home, leaving only once a month to collect groceries. There were times when he could be persuaded to tend to his yard, but only when enough notices had been taped to the front door. In fact, if he had not already paid for this vacation, it was likely the rest of his days would play out as some mundane circle of self regret.

When Linde's pale, average body fully submerged, saltwater immediately penetrated his ill-secured mask. A briny mouthful of ocean forced him to remove and refit the snorkel while simultaneously kicking leg muscles that had not been used in over a decade. And as Linde flailed in place the rest of the snorkeling platoon made their distance between themselves and the boat, and for good reason. They only had forty minutes to reach the center of the vast coral reef below.

The objective of this outing was the rare opportunity to lay eyes on the legendary Christ of the Abyss statue. Standing—or rather sunken—at a massive nine feet tall, with a weight approaching two tons, the figure of Jesus himself boasts a permanent resting place under twenty-five feet of saltwater. Some say staring into Christ's never-blinking eyes can fill a void in one's soul whether it be religious, spiritual, or otherwise. Some say just sharing the same water as the statue youthens their skin. Linde had none of these superstitions, and had no interest in the reef or its wildlife. He was simply there to touch Christ's outstretched hand and then retreat back to the safety of his home forever. But if he was ever going to get this over with, he had some swimming to do.

While waiting for someone to confirm line-of-sight of the

sunken monument, Linde decided to test the waterproofness of his Greenburg Oceanmaster by dipping it as far under the water as his arm would reach. At roughly three feet he could still read the brilliant display perfectly—10:30 a.m.—and was pleasantly surprised at the quality of the expensive watch. Interrupting his admiration for his Greenburg timepiece was an elated cry of, "Over here!" and he started floundering in that direction.

Approaching an artifact under water is not the same as on land. It does not begin very small in the distance and then slowly increase in size. It just sort of...appears. Once Linde was near enough to see the depiction of Christ, he fully understood why it donned the 'of the Abyss' title. The bronzed, barnacled statue stood on a gigantic pedestal framed by mounds of colorful coral reefs like a stitched quilt flapping in the wind. Rays of golden sun danced magnificently around the figure's outstretched arms while schools of striped fish chased each other across its waist. Particles in the water lingered and reflected the varying hues like spiritual glitter. Awe nearly froze Linde into an iceberg as he gazed onto the eternal spectacle of the Abyss. However, his bobbing stupor was forcefully thawed when he recalled the reason he was there.

Linde hastily dove straight down to try and touch Christ's hands. It was a foolish effort because not only had he never practiced diving, his life vest was still fully inflated with air. Realizing his mistake, he bobbed upwards, pinched the valve on his preserver, and squeezed every last molecule of oxygen he could from it. He then assessed his physicality and concluded that he would need to use both arms and flippered feet to create enough momentum to reach the statue. Once more, he filled his lungs with air and attempted the dive. Another miss. Again and again he struggled, but he just could not propel his body and lungs far enough.

One more try, Linde thought, allowing himself to bob and rest. *I promised.*

When he had collected himself, Linde first poked his head under the surface to ensure that he was directly above the monument. Then he calmed his breathing through proper use of the snorkel. After many large inhales and exhales his lungs were no longer burning and he was prepared to make his final plunge. He arched his back and with a great pull of his arms, his body subsided. He kicked and stroked with all of his might. His lungs reignited within his chest...fire coursed through his rubbery legs...Alas!

Linde's tired hands had gripped the oversized bronze fingers and as he held he found himself caught in Christ's unfaltering gaze. While anticipating a rush of spiritual fulfillment, his eyes instead wavered when he noticed something else lurking in the depths; something that may have uncoiled or blinked. But it was too late. Bubbles coughed from Linde's lungs and he needed to resurface before he asphyxiated himself.

On the boat ride back to Key Largo, Linde tried to make

sense of what he may or may not have witnessed beneath the Abyss. Between the statue's firm base and the crawling coral he saw the glow of a color which he could not describe. It had seen him, had moved, had known he was there.

Was it perhaps the religious awakening so many others have praised? Linde mused, sitting in cold silence the entire excursion back to shore. *Had I simply run out of air? Was I too fatigued from the swim? No...I saw it.*

———

Later that night Linde ordered a gin and tonic from the beach-side cabana at his resort while a storm brewed ominously on the Atlantic horizon. All day he had been tormented by what may have been seen that morning and thus could not sleep with fact and fiction clashing within his mind.

Since the cabana was at capacity with jubilantly drunken spouses, Linde concluded to watch the incoming weather from the seclusion of the dock. He started down the wooden planks with his drink in hand and took a moment to look skyward. A milky stroke splattered twinkling stars across an endless black canvas. Absolutely no trace of wind was present and the air surrounding felt like a calming bubble. He was captivated.

When Linde reached the end of the dock, a giggling woman with ruffled hair dashed by and he spotted a man tucking his shirt into his shorts behind the 'Rules & Regulations' board. "Nice night, huh?" the man asked as he jogged after presumably his wife. Linde chose not to respond. Instead, he took a seat on a nearby bench and gazed into the silent void alone. After draining the last sip of his drink, he turned back to not only notice the man and woman were nowhere to be seen, but the bar had also emptied as well. *Peculiar,* he thought while glancing at his expensive watch, revealing it was only 10:30 p.m.

With no complaints about the newfound silence, Linde set his glass down on the bench and continued to watch the invisible storm roll in. The surrounding night sky seemed to fall darker and darker until lightning began illuminating blackened clouds. At first it was one flash here and another flash there, but the strikes soon became more frequent. It was disturbingly beautiful to witness the power of atmospheric pressures dance above the Atlantic, and Linde was quite content with his private viewing. As more minutes rolled by the lightning struck more rapidly—incessantly—causing an uninterrupted whitish, brownish, purplish backdrop against the horizon. Then he saw it. Silhouetted against an exceptionally violent bolt was one gargantuan tentacle.

Instinctively, Linde rubbed his eyes because what he had observed could not have been real; *should* not have been real. In fact, there was no explanation other than illusions and shadows produced by the electrical current. He gazed back out into the sea and only saw the strobing outline of cumulonimbus clouds. Heavy relief was sighed and he concluded that a long day mixed with a few gin and tonics must have created the extremity in his mind.

But the lightning continued to crash and the storm continued to encroach and now something even more extraordinary caught Linde's eye. He was absolutely certain he could see multiple titanic tentacles suspended in the rain clouds. But the tentacles were not the only thing painted in the canvas of precipitation. An enormous, crustaceous claw seeming to be suffering a barrage from the cephalopodic arms also came into view. The claw swayed and opened and clasped as the tentacles attempted to grapple and gain control. *What is this madness? This...this impossible sight!* These creatures, assuming most of their bodies were still under water, would have to be hundreds, if not thousands, of feet tall!

The storm had maintained its steady advance towards shore and Linde could now hear the great booms of what he thought had been thunder. The lightning still illuminated the stage set by the clouds, but the soundwaves were curiously timed with each blow of claw on tentacle and tentacle on claw. When one would strike the other, a tumultuous bellow would blast towards Linde's seclusion on the berth. If he had not already been firmly seated, he surely would have been knocked backwards onto the dock.

The great maelstrom continued closing in and Linde could now discern the outlines of the figures attached to the awesome appendages. The first beast was humanoid in shape, but instead of arms there were three great tentacles protruding from each socket. The head was translucent and globular, but also amorphous, housing a single glowing eye that moved freely inside. The other unimaginable creation had six long, thin legs that sprang up from the ocean depths to support a largely tubular body that seemed hard like a shell. This behemoth only had one great claw while the other arm, if one could call it that, looked tiny and useless. On top of its head were many eyes attached to stalks, giving it a spider-like view of its surroundings.

Linde was involuntarily pulled to his feet as the smells of the storm now reached him. Both creations were covered thick in barnacles and dripping with submersed foliage, poisoning the sky with a putrid odor. The dense, salty air crawled up Linde's nose as he watched frozen the unthinkable clash by light of lightning. Each great blow from one monster to another produced deafening blasts and white-capped waves. They were getting ever closer—frighteningly so—yet he could not peel himself away. His instincts screamed at him to run, but his soul wanted more. An emptiness that had too long devoured his life was refilling itself in the form of a titanous brawl.

The ocean sprayed Linde's face as the great abnormalities were now near enough to be seen without the spotlight of charged electricity. Then, just like the saltwater splashing against his bare skin, something familiarly real rushed over his evaporating senses. He had to warn the residents of the resort! *But what could someone as insignificant and pathetic as me even do? Even if there was enough time to reach them, how could humans fare against such giants?* Every fiber in Linde's body insisted he flee for his life, but his mind, or what was left of it, knew that nothing could be done except stand firm and heed.

Suddenly, the humanoid cephalopod wrapped its tentacles around the impossible pincer and wrenched it free from the crab-thing's socket. The claw fell with a substantial splash and the former owner of it shrilled in torment. Then, as the tubular crustacean wailed, the first colossus pivoted into position to claim its hard-fought prize. Every tentacle deliberately and methodically curled around each groove of the defeated's husk and began to squeeze. The pressure from the constriction caused the shell-like body to crack and eventually crumble, all in tune to an otherworldly orchestra of lightning and thunder. Eventually the weakest succumbed to the tentacled prison and the struggle concluded.

Linde reeled in terror, still unable to turn away his head or even blink. What was unfolding in front of his very eyes was a maddening symphony of horrors beyond comprehension. The crustaceous beast had ended its writhing—its remaining limbs limp—and the victor began submerging the husk where it was sure to become a fitting meal. This was not a slow descent, however. The humanoid dove quickly and upset the water all around, sending a powerful wake outward.

Instantly the storm dissipated. The cloudburst returned

the calm night sky and its stars, but the monster's wave still fast approached the dock. Linde fumbled back to the bench he had initially been sitting on and clutched it with all of his might. When the swell struck, he and the shore were entirely engulfed in a wall of water. The force of the upsurge was greater than Linde's grip could ever be and it effortlessly swirled him about in its current. He flailed to find air, and soon felt the ocean enter his body while his essence escaped. Finally, after the wave had run its natural course, it left behind one lost soul face-down on a wooden dock.

Linde coughed up a lungful of saltwater and fought for control of his consciousness, followed by his own breathing. He rose to unstable feet, happy to be above ground instead of under water. But just as he thought he was free from the unfathomable nightmare, something strange called to him: a voice. It beckoned him.

Slowly, Linde dropped down to all fours and crawled to the edge of the dock. At first everything was as if it had never been, with hardly a ripple in the dark sea. Then he looked outward to find only a pitch-black sheet with calm constellations strewn about. He had never seen a horizon so glasslike. Finally, he looked at the planks of the dock; all bone dry except for him.

Baffled, Linde peered one last time into the ocean to ensure nothing but blackness peered back. *Wait,* he thought, *what is that?* It was faint, at first, resembling an illuminated fissure of inconceivable colors deep below. Colors that did not have names or definition in any Earthly tongue. Then it spread and spread and kept spreading until the colossal glowing eye of the tentacled horror stared directly into Linde's own, completely blinding him!

Linde soon found himself intertwined with a nothingness so vast—so immensely black—he thought it could never be punctured by light. But a light did appear. It was small and of unknown origin and he felt compelled to approach it.

Beneath the glow sat a hospital bed occupied by a terminally ill woman who strained to look up at Linde. A heart-wrenching tidal wave depressed him as he found himself once again accompanying her final moments. An envelope manifested in his hand; a surprise for their anniversary. It contained two plane tickets to Florida, and two more for an outing at Christ of the Abyss. For the first time in months she laughed and promptly nodded towards a small box on her bedside table. She struggled with the words, but was able to tell him that her gift would pair perfectly with his. Jamison reached over to retrieve the palm-sized package and opened it. Inside was a Greenburg Oceanmaster with nothing but a glowing, globular eye displayed on its face. Confused, he looked back at her to ask about the troubling watch, but the machines monitoring her heart had gone quiet. She was leaving him again.

"Release me from this hell!" he screamed into the void at the top of his lungs. "I promise to move on, to live my life to the fullest, if you just please end this torment!"

The hospital bed had now completely dissolved, along with his wife, and Linde finally accepted that he could not sulk in the dark for the rest of his days. Gradually, his entire existence began to resolve back into focus. He could see! He could hear! He could . . . taste saltwater at the tip of his tongue. Stunned, he searched every inch of that hellish water for one more second with her, but nothing was there. Just a black mirror reflecting the night sky.

A single tear fell from Linde's cheek and created a circular ripple. "She would have wanted me to carry on."

Relieved, alive, and soaking wet, Jamison Linde sauntered down the dock back towards the beach. Bizarrely, the cabana bar was again full of joyful patrons. Musicians were playing, couples were dancing, and families from a moonlit kayak tour were pulling their vessels ashore, all oblivious to the colossal and terrible events that had just occurred offshore. Mystified, Linde looked down at his waterproof watch, the final gift from his late wife, and it read 10:30 p.m.

THE LAST DROP

The sun had just swept away the last of the moon's cooling refuge, shifting the hue of Mirage from tepid blue to fevered pink. On the ground a door squeaked, a throat yawned, a toolbox rattled, and two weary boots stepped out into the early morning. Four paws followed enthusiastically.

Arf!

After locking the three wood planks she called a door, Mender leaned over and scratched her young German Shepherd behind the ears. "I know, Smoke Dog," she said. "We'll be done soon enough."

Smoke Dog tilted her head one way, then the other, her

carefree tongue flopping along for the ride. Mender smiled. Before long she straightened up, whistled urgently, and they both set down the dusty alleyway side by side.

The town of Mirage was built on a fundament that was convenient enough to migrate, yet unloved enough to abandon. Corrugated tin, fractured plywood, and torn canvas tarps made up the bulk of the dwellings, and each was held together by either frayed rope or bent nails. Nothing new; everything salvaged. From above, Mirage might resemble the look and shape of a rusty bolt—hollow at its center and jagged around its edges—which, coincidentally, was the piece of hardware Mender had just pinched from out her toolbox.

"You're early," a crusty voice commented, its owner emerging from around a cracked and splintered countertop. Water damaged. He ran his thumbs behind the straps of his frayed suspenders. "Didn't expect you 'til later."

"Not much of a choice, Teller. No one wants to miss the big show."

Teller leaned backwards against that same counter and watched Mender close a valve needing replacement. Next to her was a dog that was, in return, watching him. "You know," Teller started, "a lot of folk are still upset about your extra portion."

"That's odd," Mender grunted, turning a wrench. The old nut broke free and she began turning it by hand. "Because they sure don't mind me fixing all of their shit."

A raspy chuckle escaped Teller's throat and Smoke Dog tilted her head.

"Oh, it don't matter to me none. I'm as grateful as ever for your services." Then Teller paused. He moved closer to monitor Mender's progress, not forgetting to scratch the top of Smoke Dog's head as he passed. "I just say what I hear. Word lingers like poison nowadays, ya know?"

Mender swapped the rusty valve for a slightly less rusty one with careful precision. Only a trickle was spared. While she made the final turns of her wrench she said, "Poison, huh? Sounds like the good word of you-know-who."

This time Teller released a big wheezy laugh and slapped the side of the great water tank looming above the repair that had just been made. A bubble of air gurgled to the surface and popped.

Mender stood up slowly and wiped her forehead. "This really the last of it?"

Both watched as the ripples inside came to a still. "'Fraid so," Teller said.

The mood fell as low as the water level. Mender realized the encroaching gloom and patted Teller on the shoulder in hopes to stave it off. "Hey, at least now you won't have to worry about it dripping onto the dirt."

Teller smiled, kneeled down, and took Smoke Dog's scruff gently in his hands. "You two remind me of better days. I hope our path's cross at the Event later."

Mender lifted her toolbox and started for the exit. "We

weren't planning on it. Not a lot of friends here, if you know what I mean."

"Well," Teller said. "You'd have at least one."

Smoke Dog licked Teller's face and joined Mender at her side. Together they stepped into a brighter, starker morning and, without haste or complaint, started walking towards the next stop.

"Oh, wait!" a voice soon hailed from behind. Mender turned and saw Teller's lean body swiveling inside his baggy overalls while bumbling after them. "You forgot your canteen," he said once he caught up.

"Thank you."

Teller looked at them both and winked. "Filled 'er to the three-portion mark, but no one needs to know that."

Arf!

With goodbyes said, Mender and Smoke Dog left Teller to his banking business.

———

The morning was now hot enough to hint at how stifling the day was going to be when they arrived at Compendium—Mirage's holy compound of the self-righteous. It was perhaps the largest, most well-kempt structure in town, yet somehow the least welcoming. Especially to an outsider and her dog.

"You're late," Preacher scolded as Mender entered the courtyard. There was a dried-up fountain and an array of flowerbeds filled with bleached stones and colorful imitations of in-bloom plants. "But patience guides me."

Mender sighed a heavy sigh. A trailing tenant raked hers and Smoke Dog's footprints away while they approached the main building. "Had to stop at Teller's first."

"Indeed," Preacher said, then gestured her inside. He glared at the dog as it followed.

Beneath the tall ceiling of Compendium's main structure were many rows of chairs leading up to a lectern. Dotted holes in the sheet metal above bathed the room in strands of yellow light while dust particles danced from beam to beam. Beside the lectern, to where Mender was being led, was a great marble bowl resting on a waist-high podium. A cast iron cover once intended for manholes rested on its rim.

"The lock has been damaged," Preacher reported. "It must be mended before this morning's service."

"Yes, sir," Mender said sharply, then set her toolbox down equally as so. She pulled out a large file coated in brown rust and jammed it inside the damaged shackle of the twisted padlock. A quick pry at the right angle popped it free.

However, Mender was not expecting the old lock to be quite so frail and she lost her balance, bumping her hips into the massive bowl. Water sloshed inside and a brief stream squeezed from under the manhole cover. Smoke Dog's head tilted in interest as it all splashed onto the floor.

"Be careful!" Preacher scolded. He rushed over to the podium and steadied the bowl. After the wobbling stopped,

Mender conceded, "Sorry."

Preacher raised an eyebrow and asked, "Sorry? *Sorry?* Do not pretend you understand the value of what lies within this font."

"I was just—"

"Help me with this."

The interruption startled Mender, but she obliged out of nature. Together they lifted the heavy slab of iron and leaned it against the nearby lectern. While they were crouched, Smoke Dog reared her front paws onto the rim of the bowl and started lapping.

"Stop that mongrel!" cried Preacher, and with great intent he swooped over with a raised hand.

Mender commanded a sharp whistle and the dog, ears flat against its head, retreated to her side before any damage could be dealt.

"Are you insane? She's just thirsty like the rest of us!"

Preacher, shame absent from his face, lowered the offending arm and reached it behind the lectern. Out came a clear plastic gallon container once meant for cow's milk. There was a cross drawn on the side with a black marker.

"Insanity would be delegating precious drinking water to such a godless beast; much less *holy* water."

Mender watched with disdain as Preacher poured clean water from the container back into the oversized bowl. "You forget that my extra portion is the reason I'm here fixing your lock. A deal I made with the entire town. At least Smoke Dog drinks it while all Compendium does is splash it on people's faces."

Preacher was unfazed. When the font was topped off, he snapped the lid back on his sacred container and put it away. "A dog and dogma can hardly sit under the same umbrella. When the time comes, only the righteous will be rewarded."

The dog whined. One of Mender's hands instinctively scratched the top of its head while the other disappeared inside of her toolbox. It came back holding a brand-new padlock still inside its original packaging. A prized possession.

"If you're so righteous," Mender said, tossing the generous gift at Preacher, "then why do you need this?"

———

After more miserable stops with more miserable people—Cobbler, Digger, Tailor—Mender and her dog found themselves in a darker corner of Mirage. Darker not because it sat in the shade, which would have been preferred, but because of the clientele. The building in question was right on the edge of town, where entrants could sneak in from both inside and outside the limits. If asked, no one officially came to this establishment, including Mender, but she had made her promise to fix what needed fixing.

A little bell dinged inside the dusty hovel as two expected guests entered. One carried a toolbox and the other their tail between their legs. "It's okay, girl. Let's just get this over with."

A woman drifted out into the open from who-knows-where with an eager smile across her face. She wore an old driver's cap—a relic from when there were cars—and a nicely fitted grey suit—a relic from when there were offices. The tightness of the suit did little to hide the robustness of her body, a questionable sight in such times.

"What a pleasant surprise!" exclaimed the attendant. "Come to place your bet for the Event?"

The dog whimpered at the tone of the greeting. Mender rolled her eyes. "You know damn well why I'm here, Bookkeeper. It's because you called on me."

The smile on Bookkeeper's face waned, but her bright eyes held firm. "Ah, right. Of course I did. Follow me."

They went into a room not visible from the entryway that housed a staircase leading down into the earth. Four boots and four paws descended the rickety planks and stood before a makeshift vault under the light of a single hanging lamp. The rusty door sat crooked.

"Had another break in last night," Bookkeeper sighed. Mender walked across the gravel floor and inspected its edges. Bookkeeper kept speaking. "This is the most successful yet. He managed to get the door cracked before I bashed his knees in with a bat. Oh how I howled as I watched him crawl back into the desert!"

Mender, choosing to ignore the unabashedly morbid tale, said, "Looks like you need a new hinge."

Bookkeeper narrowed her eyes at the lack of reaction she received. She put her hands on her healthy hips and shuffled over. "Can you fix it," she said, rather than ask.

"I can," replied Mender, "but I'm going to have to remove the door."

If there was one thing that could shake the wiliness of Bookkeeper's comportment, it was the thought of someone bearing witness to what lay inside her vault. "Is there no other way?"

"Not if you want it to last, which I expect you will after today."

Bookkeeper walked back to the staircase and listened upwards for loitering footsteps or the ding of her bell. After a quiet moment she glanced back at Mender and nodded.

With respect to the client and her own craftsmanship, Mender removed the vault door with careful hands. Her solar-charged drill pulled the rusty screws from the top and bottom hinges, of which only two snapped, then she slid the heavy slab aside. A cellar beyond Mender's greatest imagination filled its place.

Arf!

"Arf is right, girl."

Almost stunned in place, Mender gazed upon the vault's offerings. Shelves and shelves of bottled waters, energy drinks, and sodas sat dusted with their original labels facing forward. Plastic tubs with large tags reading "Jerky" and "Chips" and "Candy Bars" were stacked on one another like colorful building blocks. A large table had hundreds of jars of red and green and orange things floating in vinegars and brines. All things she'd never thought she'd see again.

"All right, all right," Bookkeeper announced, rushing back to Mender with conviction. "Show's over. I didn't call you here to gawk."

Swallowing the brief moment of salivation down, Mender shook her head clear. She kneeled and rifled through her toolbox for some newish hinges and screws. And though she already knew the reply, she felt she had to say, "You know, this stuff could help a lot of people."

Bookkeeper burst into a cynical cackle. "You're cute, kid. Wrong...but cute. You of all people should know that the world doesn't work like that. Never has."

Mender was on her feet now, reinforcing the splintered door frame first with thicker screws. Bookkeeper's audacity was eating at her. "You know what's happening later today. You could do a lot of good."

The now understandably healthy woman leaned against the cave-like wall next to Mender, almost hovering above her. "Let me give you a bit of advice, hm? Gratitude around here lasts about as long as a cool breeze. It feels good for a moment, but once that heat comes back, well, that's when they come knocking. Then they'll knock and knock and knock until they take all the breeze you have. And that's when they get angry. People like you and me, we have to cool ourselves, you hear?"

The dog at Mender's side gave a whine while she herself sighed. As much as she did not like to admit it, Bookkeeper was right. They *were* similar. One had skills while the other had resources. And no matter how much of each either of them offered, they would always be asked for more. And more. And more...

"Speaking of today," Bookkeeper continued, her saleslady pep returning in full, "Have you placed your bet yet?"

The new hinges had been fastened to the frame and Mender was moving onto the door. "I don't gamble."

"You might change your tune when you hear what the prize is."

Mender rolled her eyes. "I'll hear it."

The shark bared her teeth with a wide smile. "It's a fifty-fifty raffle. Everyone wages a portion in exchange for a time slot. The person who guesses the correct time walks away with half the winnings. Of course, I'll keep the other half for going through the trouble."

The repaired door was lifted and set against the newish hinges. Mender only offered up a, "Hmm," while tamping in the new pins.

"Now I still got 12:46 open....and a 12:52...oh, also an 11:24, but that seems a bit early if you ask me."

"No thanks."

"Oh, come on. We both know you've got an extra portion sloshin' around in that canteen of yours. Think of it as free money!"

Mender looked at Smoke Dog. Her ears went flat against her head. "It's not my portion."

"Shame," Bookkeeper said, shaking her head and clicking her tongue. "Nearly the whole town is on this list. The winner would have enough supplies to ditch Mirage and start a fresh life...if she were so inclined."

Once the vault door was hinged and secured, Mender and her dog were followed back up the stairs by Bookkeeper, who checked the craftsmanship many times beforehand. When they turned into the main lobby a bell dinged. A local entered wearing an unusually spotless pair of boots.

"Ah, Cobbler!" Bookkeeper exclaimed, arms wide while bypassing Mender and her companion. "Welcome!"

"Came to place me bet," he said with a sandpaper voice. "Whaddya got left?"

"I'm glad you stopped in! Let's see, 12:46 is still open... and 12:52...oh, also 11:24, but that seems a bit early if you ask me."

Cobbler followed Bookkeeper towards her counter, shouldering Mender on the way. "You and that mutt's the reason I'm in here," he muttered.

Mender's head fell heavy. She had fixed a table clamp at Cobbler's shop not one hour ago and here he was condemning her. And for what? Eight extra ounces of water? At this point she just wanted to go home and curl into a ball and let it all pass by. But Bookkeeper was right. Someone would eventually knock on her door. Then the next day. And again the day after that. Maybe it was time to cool herself.

She glanced down at Smoke Dog, remembering Teller's generosity from that morning, and smirked.

"Actually, Cobbler, I was here first."

———

Just around noon, at the edge of the lake Mirage was built around, Mender drove her rickety umbrella into the cracked earth and sat down beneath its protective shadow. It was hot now. Boiling hot. Smoke Dog walked a small circle, lay in the shaded dust, and began panting.

Mender unscrewed the top of her now two-portion canteen and took a large pull. Then she unpopped a collapsible dog bowl and filled it with half of what was left.

"I know, girl," she said as Smoke Dog whined at how little was presented. "But I think I have a plan."

All around the lake the citizens of Mirage gathered with chairs that were once meant for lawns and umbrellas that were once meant for rain. Besides Mender, not many came alone. Most had clans or cliques or clubs that they traveled in and nearly all had one or more slips of white paper held covetously between dry, cracked fingers.

Today really was the day, Mender thought to herself, scanning the people piling in. Literally everyone had shown up—Digger, Tailor, Cobbler. Teller waved at her from afar, looking almost like a child inside of his baggy overalls. Even Preacher had bothered to show his face, albeit without his convent.

Mender looked at an old pocket watch she had restored in her free time: 11:56. "Looks like Bookkeeper was right, 11:24 was a bit early."

Smoke Dog sneezed.

"By the way, where is that old shark?"

But just as Mender thought it out loud she spotted the sharply dressed woman standing only twenty feet away holding an immaculate polka dot umbrella in one hand and a funny sort of clock in the other. It looked like a black brick with many bright green numbers bursting from the front— hours, minutes, seconds, milliseconds. It was an antique Greenburg GPS clock; mint condition, perfectly accurate. Mender had seen one before, but never in working order. She would have to keep a sharp eye on it.

"Feeling confident?" a voice called out.

Mender looked up from the clock to see Bookkeeper smiling widely at her. "We'll just have to see," she replied back.

The loan shark returned her gaze to the center of the ring of people. The sun was directly above now—12:05—and the water's edge was rapidly receding. At only a few inches deep, there was no sense in wasting energy to collect what remained of the lake so the whole town agreed to watch it disappear in peace.

That is, until one citizen decided to turn the Event into profit. Now all of Mirage sat shifting and groaning as time either passed too quickly or not quickly enough. Each minute that went by ruined another's hope at the jackpot. When 12:17 struck, Tailor threw his slip onto the dirt and stomped on it. Mender could not help but smile.

12:30 came and Mender placed a hand on top of Smoke Dog's head. This perked up her triangle ears and reminded her long tongue of how thirsty it was. Heavy panting began.

Mender glanced at Bookkeeper's clock again. 12:33. Another groan from out in the crowd sparked and snuffed and all became pins and needles because not much water was left. Maybe three feet from edge to edge and only an inch or so deep. And though the sun was thirsty, Mender held on to one who was thirstier.

12:40 now.

To Mender's surprise, Preacher was the one to throw his ticket down this time. At his feet was a healthy pile of others—all losers. It looked like someone else would be drinking holy water tonight.

12:42.

Mender went over the rules in her head one last time. Bet your portion, choose a time slot, then Bookkeeper would call out the winner once the lake officially dried up. Nothing specifically referring to the sun. Good.

12:44.

She kept one eye on the clock while the other found

Cobbler. He was sitting across the lake from her, paper in hand, staring her down. He knew her time and she knew his. Her blood was about to boil when she noticed the silly way in which he sat to keep his pristine boots under the shade of his chair. She would relish this sight in her victory.

12:45:20.

Would Mender miss Mirage? Maybe Teller. But she could thank him later on. Come back for him, even. As for right now, she was taking Bookkeeper's advice: it was high time she took care of herself. And it just so happened that Mender's time was right now.

12:45:50.

"Hey girl. Are ya thirsty?"

Smoke Dog jumped up to attention, wagging her tail and panting profusely.

Arf!

"Well, go get it!"

At exactly 12:46, the time at which Mender had bet her one extra portion, a young German Shepherd flew to the center of Mirage and lapped up what was left of its water.

Every last drop.

MAN, KIND
The Grand Hotel
OOO CIRCLE OOO
VALOUR
MY DEAR MARGARET
All You Can Eat!
THIS AMERICAN LIFE
BOXES THE GAME
the NIGHT SHIFT
THE LINE
JAMISON LINDE SCUBA PASS
COMING HOME
S.P.
The LAST DROP OO
LOST VEGAS
THE MOTHERS EYE
POMO

HEIRLOOM

When I received the old man's letter I was both confused and pleasantly surprised. I had not heard from him in decades, and was almost certain he had passed away, yet somehow now in my possession was signed and stamped proof of his existence.

Like the rain clouds above, I hovered over the mailbox until the mailman doubled back his route on the opposite side of the street. The scribbled address to my name had been so daunting I had not realized the absence of all my spatial awareness. Awkwardly, I waved at him and he waved back, then a sudden snap of thunder kindly reminded me why I had rushed outside in the first place. Since neither snow nor rain did not apply to me, I tucked the letter between bills and coupons and scuttled back up the driveway.

Inside I examined the envelope thoroughly. The front contained my name and address at the center, and only his initial—*M*—on the top left. The back was sealed with a small, golden sticker depicting a poorly embossed tiger, perhaps dulled by its journey. I turned the mysterious parchment over in my hands about fifty times before finally sliding a letter opener through the gold seal, revealing a brief, handwritten note.

> *Dear Young Liam,*
>
> *I'm sorry to inconvenience you on this twenty-third day of April, however, if your time allows, I have an urgent request. Could you visit my cottage for an evening? Please check that water and electricity still flow, and ensure that the animals are cared for. Visit my primary residence first to round up overnight supplies. Also, feel free to use the truck. My keys are on the hook to the left of the door.*
>
> *P.S. If you find fulfillment in one night, you are most welcome to stay another.*
>
> *~M*

I reread the vague inquiry three more times while scratching my head. His arrangement of words seemed almost cryptic in manner, and left much for interpretation. I knew of this "cottage" he was referring to and, to be blunt, it was more of a rusty shack in the middle of the woods than an actual home for vacationing. The primary residence he spoke of was the old house down the way from the one I grew up in, but I had not been back home since my mother's funeral. And the animals he mentioned must have been in reference to his old Jack Russell Terrier and grey tabby cat, but there was no way they had survived this long.

Troubled, I set the letter down and collapsed into a nearby recliner. As a lighthouse surveys an empty ocean, so too I swiveled my chair around a devoid, darkened house. "Young Liam," I mused to myself. That was a nickname I had not heard in a long time. He had called me that when the top of my head barely came up to his waist. Now I am nearing my fourth decade and those words have been absent from my life since I left. In fact, I sighed, not many shared words with me at all nowadays.

I picked up the letter and read it once more aloud. The request was for just one evening, it said. I glanced around my desolate house again. Aside from the chair I was sitting in, there was one couch, one table, an aging TV, and many walls that hung no frames. Nothing of pertinence waited for me here. It was as empty and aimless as the one who occupied it. Maybe, I considered, a night in the woods was just what

I needed.

During the plane ride back out west to Oregon—to home—I fell into a deep dream. Various flashpoints of my childhood, almost like a slideshow, jumped from the darkest caverns of my brain. I was ten again, watching a car drive down the road from my house window. My mom came up from behind and placed her warm hands on my shoulders. "We still have each other," she told me, but I knew life would only become harder.

The next instance showed my mom hunched over, trying to slide black shoes onto her feet. She was getting ready for her second job as a waitress and would be gone for another twelve hours. Before she exited through the front door, she kissed my forehead and told me to have fun today. Her car disappeared, revealing a rusty Chevrolet pickup waiting for me at the end of the driveway. I sauntered head-down towards it. The old man was behind the wheel. "Happy Birthday, kid," he said, then handed me a small, hand-whittled tiger. He had carved it himself. I then found myself in my bedroom later that night. I was lining up wooden toys to admire. There was a wild dog, an armadillo, a mountain lion, and a leopard. I slid the new tiger into the formation with my finger.

The final instance flung me to my final year in high school. I was wearing an all-black suit that was too big and staring into an open casket. I was frozen. Everyone that came to pay their respects to my mother also came to give me a hug. I hated that. I had to pretend to be happy to see them when the only thing I wanted was to be alone with her one last time. Once everyone left, so did the casket, and I stood deserted facing the front of the church. When I finally turned to leave, the old man was sitting on the farthest pew from me at the back of the room. We exchanged eyes and he nodded to me silently. That simple gesture gave me the most comfort I had felt all week. It was also the last time I ever saw him.

I awoke in a cold sweat to the captain giving her static-filled update over the plane's intercom—thanks again for flying Sahara Air and we would soon be landing. As the aircraft descended, I pondered over my dream. My hazy recollections of my time with the old man were flooding back with pure clarity. I really had spent a lot of time with him while my mother was working one of her jobs. He would typically take me out fishing, on a hike, or deep into the forest where he would teach me about nature, the animals that occupied it, and our responsibility as humans to look after it all. He taught me practical skills and gave me the knowledge to respect the only planet we live on. Then I remembered the small wooden animals he would carve for me on my birthdays. I had always looked forward to those.

After the plane landed, I had a car drop me off in front of my mother's old house. I had no idea who lived there now; I just wanted to see it. It looked mostly the same save for a few new plants growing in an updated window box. The same window I had watched her disappear from so many times.

But before the wave of nostalgia could consume me, I started down the sidewalk with my duffel bag in one hand and the letter in the other.

When I reached the old man's house, I realized I had never been inside. I was chuckling to myself while turning the squeaky door handle when suddenly a small dog burst from the opening and sprinted out into the yard. What startled me most was not the creature's unexpected welcome, but that it looked identical to the Jack Russell Terrier the old man had had thirty years ago! True it could have been the offspring of an offspring, but the likeness was uncanny.

I entered the house to grab some supplies while the dog did its emergency business in the yard. It had quickly become apparent that no one had actually *lived* in this home for many years. Every surface was caked with an inch-thick layer of dust and the only light came from sparse beams slipping through cracks in the blinds. I found an old light switch in the hallway and pushed the top button in. One bulb instantly popped and the rest flickered slowly into existence.

Once I found the kitchen I sifted through empty cupboards in search of food for my overnight retreat. Pots, pans, plates, silverware; completely void of things to eat. Next I tried the fridge, but immediately closed it before vomiting from the stench that tried to escape. The smell must have attracted the dog because it ran back into the house and started sniffing around the kitchen until finally pawing at the pantry door. There was good news inside: somewhat stocked. I grabbed a couple of soup cans, some expired oat bars, and a package of water bottles. Enough to hold me over for a night or two.

Before I turned to exit, two brand new bags of pet food caught my eye. The dog yelped up at me from the floor. "You want some?" I asked. The terrier did a quick spin indicating yes so I grabbed both bags to take with us and noticed something. Only one of the bags was for dogs while the other was for their feline counterparts. The letter *did* mention taking care of animals, plural.

After searching all the habitable areas of the house, I found no traces of the old man's old grey cat—if it was even alive. The idea seemed far-fetched, considering the uncanny likeness of the dog, but I half-expected to find another exact copy eager to meet me. Alas, there was none. And since the cottage would be significantly harder to find in total darkness, I decided to just leave out food and water in the kitchen and head out with the dog. The truck keys were on the hook to the left of the door, right where the letter said they would be, and we exited through the front.

When I opened the driver's side of the same rusty Chevrolet pickup from my childhood, the dog leapt in as if it had been anticipating this ride all day. The pup brought an unexpected smile to my face as I threw the supplies, pet food, and my duffel bag into the truck's bed. Next I slid into the driver seat. For a brief moment I was ten years old again. I recalled sitting on the old man's lap as he let me steer the old

Chevy while he worked the pedals. Once we drove by some old ladies sitting on a bench in town. We honked, waved, and laughed as their feathers ruffled at the sight of a child driving.

The key sputtered the ancient engine into a gurgling idle as if I had awoken an elderly bear in the middle of hibernation. I rolled down the window. The evening breeze was warm and mellow and supplied some much-needed fresh air before putting the musty truck in gear. I pulled the lever next to the steering wheel down and watched the indicating arrow scroll across the dash into the drive position. Then, just as I glanced behind the truck bed to make sure I had turned off all the lights in the house, a small shadow leapt through the window I had just rolled down and landed on my lap. Startled, I found a figure licking its paw. A grey tabby! The ash colored feline gave me an acknowledging blink, hopped next to the dog on the passenger seat, and they both waited patiently for me to set off for the cottage.

During our back road commute to the forest, I pondered the old man's request to take care of the animals. I probably should have just left the cat and dog at his house, but they had both seemed very eager to tag along with me, as if they were anticipating something. My thoughts faded once we arrived at the edge of the wood and I could see the deep orange sky behind the blackened treeline. The terrier stretched its body and leaned its front paws on the dashboard, appearing extra alert, while the cat remained content licking its front paw and running it across its head. Darkness came frighteningly quick while the truck grumbled beneath the canopy and I suddenly found myself glad to have some furry companionship.

When I pulled up to the cottage, I saw that it, too, looked exactly how it did when I was little: a compact box of plywood and corrugated sheet metal dropped in the middle of nowhere. The textbook definition of a shack.

I opened the Chevy's door and both animals hopped out behind me. Under the dying red light of evening I grabbed the supplies from the truck bed and brought them over to the shack's entry. There was another key on the ring that did not belong to the pickup so I assumed it was to this flimsy metal handle hanging by stripped screws. I inserted the key, turned the knob, and unstuck the water-expanded wood from its moldy frame with a *fwump!* Both cat and dog dashed across my feet and I followed them in.

The trailer-sized single-room shack had not changed one bit. To my immediate right was a small wireframe bed accompanied by an end table, to my left was a small kitchenette, which included a sink, cupboards, a stovetop, and a fridge, and in the back was a wooden desk with a chair nestled underneath and a lamp resting on top. There was one square window in the center of each wall. Since I had only minutes left of sun, I figured I should quickly open them to move some air through the stagnant room.

First I opened the window above the sink by pulling the shade back and pinching the mechanism to slide the glass upwards. Then I opened the one above the bed. I enjoyed the cool scent of pine and bark flowing past me as I shuffled over to the window at the back of the dwelling. I leaned over and with both hands pulled the curtains from the center. What I saw on the other side of the glass nearly sent me backwards onto my head. Right there, looking directly into the shack, was a full-grown cougar. I instinctively froze, yet the animal did not seem interested in me, like it was looking *for* something instead of *at* something.

Shortly after thoroughly scanning my living space, the cougar silently retired back into the forest. I turned on a lamp and began unloading the supplies from my bag . That's when I realized the animal had probably just smelled my unobtainable food and was hoping for an easy meal. With my mind now settled, I opened the cupboards to put my supplies away. Funny, they were just as empty as the old man's home. Could the cougar really have smelled the packaged food in my bag?

Shrugging, I preemptively pinched my nose and dared open the fridge to reveal that that, too, was empty. There was an expected musty odor, but at least it was on. Then, while I was loading in the water bottles, I realized something else had been off about that particular cougar. Not that it had been so close to the shack while I was inside, but that it was unlike any mountain lion I had ever seen. The large cat had a tannish coat typical to its species, but instead of an all-white chin and underbelly, it was grey. "Must have fallen into the mud," I told myself as I placed the last bottle inside the fridge and closed it.

I slept rather soundly that night with the old man's cat curled up between my legs and the dog against my torso. I awoke fully rested sometime after sunrise to bright beams of light framing the curtains. After I slid the curtain above the bed open, I made sure to check for more visitors before lifting the glass. The morning air smelled of fresh spring flowers and windswept pines. The perfect combination. I took a quiet moment to appreciate every stimulating scent before cracking into an expired oat bar. Then I noticed the cat and dog staring up at me with hungry eyes. "Sorry guys!" I said, immediately recalling the pet food I forgot in the truck.

I slipped on my t-shirt, jeans, and shoes and opened the door of the shack. As soon as there was enough space between the door and the frame, the terrier bolted through the gap and disappeared behind some trees. "Shit!" I cried out, not knowing if I should chase the dog, or if it would eventually come back on its own. Deciding that I would feed the cat first, I grabbed the food from the truck, filled a bowl, then began scouting the immediate area. It was not long before I came to the realization that I had not known what the old man named his pets. I improvised, shouting, "Here doggy!" while walking the perimeter of the shack.

When I reached the far side of the cottage, I was abruptly introduced to the most fear my body was capable of sustaining. I stumbled backwards over the crunchy underbrush until my back was pressed firmly into the sheet metal siding. I remained motionless, silent. Mere feet away from me were three creatures that would never, *could* never, be found standing together. Huddled there was an adolescent Bengal tiger, an unbelievably rare and beautiful snow leopard, and the unique cougar from the night before. All three of them were positioned as if they had been in deep conversation before I rudely interrupted.

The impossible trio turned their heads to face me, but, to my surprise, their teeth were not bared and their ears were not folded back. They were completely neutral to my presence. I took a few deep breaths and positioned myself to flee when my missing dog burst from the woods. It was chasing a creature equal to its size right into the opening between myself and the gigantic cats. The terrier barked and dove onto the young tiger cub, leaving me with the responsibility to explain to the old man how his dog was killed and eaten. But instead of turning the pup into an easy meal, the tiger cubling rolled onto its back and sprawled out—a vulnerable position for cats. I rubbed my eyes in disbelief. They were playing!

How adorably baffling. What other secrets had the old man kept from me? Had he meant for me to witness this? Despite the many questions I had swirling in my mind, it was time for me to carefully, and slowly, back away from this bizarre scene. But just as I was about to make my escape, I saw the three large cats lift their attention above my eyes and to the shack's window. My head followed their line of sight and

I, too, saw the old man's grey cat perched behind the glass. I am aware that humans enjoy projecting their own behaviors onto animals, but these gestures—nods and blinking eyes—resembled unmistakable notions of friendship.

This was my chance to flee. Quickly, I scooped up the terrier from its orange-and-black-striped friend and dashed around the front of the shack. Once I was safely inside, I slammed the door and initiated every lock and fortification I could find. I would not be torn apart by gigantic beasts today! Then, when I reached the window that the old man's cat was perched in, I found nothing but an empty glen. Good. I pulled the curtain shut and let out a sigh of relief.

A short time later, a scratch came from the door, followed by a faint growl. I ignored it for fear of my own life. But after a while it was clear the sounds were too soft to come from a full-grown animal, so I built up my courage and peered through the door's small cutout window. It was the tiger cub! It wanted inside the shack, I presumed, with desire to visit the pup.

Some ill-advised sympathy was beginning to form inside of me. Before I could make any rash decisions, I glanced through each of the windows once more to ensure no adult predators were waiting to make me their dinner. The old man once told me that big cats had mastered the art of camouflage. He'd always say, "If you ever spot a mountain lion, it spotted you an hour ago." But surely the radiant coats of these out-of-habitat animals would not blend in so seamlessly to the deep greens and browns of a temperate forest? Either way, the cub did not cease chuffing and clawing at the door.

Finally, my heart gave in. If this animal was lost, or had just been abandoned at my feet, I could not in good conscience let it face the trials of nature. I strategically grabbed a stainless steel ladle from a drawer and held it high above my head. Then, using extreme caution, I cracked the door open. A small, yet comparatively huge paw slipped through the gap and a pink nose followed. Suddenly, a fluffy mass of orange, black, and white fur was inside the shack with myself and the old man's pets. The dog excitedly resumed their play session until the tiger cub eventually jumped onto the bed to approach the grey housecat. I watched nervously, as felines are very territorial, while the two brushed up against each other. There was a moment of pause followed by the cat licking a few out of place tufts on the cub's head. I could not believe what I was witnessing.

The animals settled in and I took one last glance of caution out the windows to confirm my corner of the forest was indeed empty. At this point it was already after noon and my anxiety was interrupted by my rumbling stomach. This seemed as good a time to eat as any, so I cracked open a tin can of vegetable stew and dumped it into a small pot.

The shack was so small that I could stir my meal while seated on the bed. As I waited for a light boil, I felt a warm, wet piece of low-grit sandpaper scrape from the bottom of my jaw and up to my ear. I jumped so high that my head hit the ceiling! Frantically searching for the thing trying to tear my face off, I soon realized the culprit was a tiger's tongue. *It must be hungry,* I thought. I was not sure at what age a large cat weened from milk, but the cat food I had brought along would have to do. I laid out three bowls, two with cat food and one with dog food, and watched the perplexing arrangement of animals feast together.

I sat back on the bed and enjoyed my own meal along with them. When they finished, tongue baths were in order. The three unlikely friends took their time cleaning their fur and eventually curled up beside me for an afternoon nap. As if on cue, sleep crept up on my own eyes and I joined them.

When I awoke I had no bearing on the time. How long had I been sleeping? A faint glow of deep amber split through the curtain's gap on the west side of the shack. I pulled the shade and saw the sunset marinating the treetops. Small beams of orangish-reddish light reached the forest floor, but quickly dissipated as hungry darkness devoured them. Just as the letter had predicted, it looked like I would be spending another night in the shack.

My attention returned to the groggy triad of small animals. The tiger cub yawned, stretched out to twice its length, and hopped off the bed. Just like before, it scratched at the door to request passage once again. After some thought, I decided to let the small tiger out and it disappeared into the darkening wood.

Once I resumed my spot on the bed, both of the old

man's animals were not only awake, but restlessly pacing around the limited space of the shack. I did not know what had them so active so I chose to lay back down on the shorter width of the bed with my legs hanging off the edge. My head fell to the right and I suddenly noticed an object on the floor between the wall and the bedframe. It looked like a small black box or package that, judging by its position, had been knocked off the bed by one of the animals when I arrived. Using my index and middle finger, I fished out the object and examined it. It was a tattered, leather-bound notebook. Curiosity got the best of me. I cracked it open to reveal the same handwriting as the letter I had received only a few days earlier.

February 24th

All these years and the forest still manages to surprise me. A cub was born today! And at this season! It was truly magical to behold. The parents are very proud and it will grow to be a strong leader.

March 3rd

Hunters again. Need to be more careful. It only takes one careless mistake to lose everything. My life's work would be gone in an instant.

March 24th

I have fallen ill. This place needs a guardian. It is too important. Over the years I have spent more and more time here because it needed it...I needed it. I rarely visit home anymore, but a hospital would only draw unwanted questions. I can't be absent for too long. The forest shrinks every day. Must stay warm and dry to overcome this myself. If something were to happen . . . Charlie and Sam would never understand.

April 6th

My condition is getting worse. I will need a successor. Perhaps Young Liam. He has a kind heart and always shared my passion for this forest. I think back fondly of our time together. The fatherless boy filled a void in this childless man's soul.

But if I tell him the truth, he'll never come. No one would. This place . . . this place needs to be shown, not told. Need to devise a letter to get him here. It will only take a single day for him to understand.

I dropped the emotive diary flat onto my lap and

slammed it shut. Did the old man deceive me into coming here after thirty years of estrangement, knowing very well I could have been mauled earlier that day? This was madness! In a rage, I shoved my belongings into my duffel bag and looked at the now-abandoned pets. I told Charlie and Sam that we were leaving and clicked off the lamp. Charlie wagged his tail by the door as any dog would, but Sam was more elusive. I tried to scoop her up as she darted from surface to surface. With one last effort, I snagged the cat mid-jump and bumped my head against the west window, inadvertently knocking down the attached curtains.

To my utter disbelief, yet another implausible animal was looking through the glass. My eyes caught its own and it gazed at me intently. I frantically scavenged my brain for the correct identification of the hypnotic beast. It was another large cat, *that* I could be sure of, but one of which I could not completely classify. Its fur was the most brilliant burnt gold I had ever witnessed on a mammal; so saturated it glowed in the absence of light. Perhaps some sort of a leopard? No, the markings were too large and too perfectly geometric. The golden fur was broken by a flawless grid of deep black hexagons that only created more contrast in the unique coat. It must be a jaguar! A jaguar, yes, but one unlike any I had ever seen in a zoo or textbook.

Its stoic stare held me in place. This animal was the most beautiful thing I had ever witnessed and it was beckoning me. Asking me to...actually I was not sure what it was asking.

I cannot specifically speak feline—tabby or otherwise. Yet, somehow, I just *knew* that this creature wanted me to follow it. To trust it.

I gathered up what remained of my sanity, and the two pets, and left the shack to meet the mysterious glowing feline. Even though this scenario went against the grain of everything I had ever learned in my life, I marched on. I rushed across the crunchy ground with a cat under one arm and a dog under the other. Once I reached the far side of the shack, I found the jaguar still waiting patiently for me. It turned slowly and entered the woods. Charlie, Sam, and I followed.

As we trudged along, the forest became denser and darker. The plant life had become so overwhelmingly thick that the very air around us changed. Even the strongest ray of light would not have been able to shine down here. Luckily, the jaguar in front of me was so brilliant it doubled as a guiding star. It was soon clear to me that I was following a predetermined path set by the large cat. Any misstep and I would have found myself lost forever.

Finally, we broke through a threshold of moss-coated branches that revealed an opening both vast and secluded. Tree trunks, leaves, bushes, and vines wrapped around each other to create a dome-shaped clearing capable of blocking all light—and prying eyes—from the outside. Yet mine could still see everything as clear as day. All around me were various unidentifiable plants, fungi, and insects that, together, illuminated the dome in a rainbow of colors that flickered like a living campfire. It was beyond magical.

Only when I finished reveling in the natural glow of evolution did I notice the sheer number of species congregating inside this temple among trees. Every single animal found their designated place within a number of ascending rings, attentions focused on the center of the living dome. Without pause, the jaguar led me to, and then through, the huddled wildlife. On the edge I saw the cougar, snow leopard, and tiger, along with its cub, but the further in we ventured, the more diverse the creatures became. There was a group of some sort of half-horse-half-zebras, strange horned antelopes, and frightening, dog-looking beasts with stripes on the rear halves of their bodies. Wait! I recognized the latter from a childhood interest in endangered animals thanks to the old man. Those were Thylacines, or, Tasmanian tigers! But those all disappeared decades ago. And the others—

"Oh my," I gasped once it hit me.

That peculiar zebra had to be a long-extinct quagga, and the antelope would have to be a bubal hartebeest. Then my eyes nearly escaped my head as I noticed more and more supposedly abolished creatures. There were passenger pigeons perched high above me, flightless great auks and dodos sitting in nests on the ground, small, doglike warrahs standing alert, and even an armored anteater called a pangolin standing on hind legs with its narrow nose to the air. Either this domed haven somehow resided in a century prior to my own, or I was standing among the last remaining specimens of each of these animals. But that would mean...

I looked back at the cougar, the snow leopard, the tiger, and her cub. Snow leopards were already on the brink of extinction, but mountain lions were not. Whether you call them cougars, panthers, or pumas, the population of those wild cats is actually thriving. But then I remembered a particular cousin of the species that was direly fighting for numbers. A branch that had grey undersides instead of white. The endangered Florida panther.

Then what about the tiger I had thought to be an adolescent? At first I, like anyone, assumed that any orange tiger must be a Bengal, but these new circumstances brought intense gravity to my realizations. The mother and her cub were not Bengal tigers at all. They were far too small. The two had to be Bali tigers—a tragically over-hunted species in the 1940s and 50s. A tragedy that explained the old man's excitement over the birth in his journal. But how could all of this come to be? How could all of these animals have found sanctuary in this very forest?

I pushed these mind-boggling questions to the back of my head as soon as the golden jaguar revealed to me what was at the center of this impossible ring of wildlife. He was lying there with his head propped up on a barkless log, covered in large, foreign-to-this-forest leaves. It was the old man himself.

He coughed, straining his weakened neck to look up at me. I kneeled down to get closer. He had the look of a man about to enter the next life; conserving every ounce of energy for his final words. Words that exhaled themselves as he spoke. "Young Liam. Do you understand?"

I nodded.

"Protect them," he pleaded, "until the world is ready."

With his dying request he held out a shaky hand for me to take. As I positioned both of mine around his, he dropped a small object into my palm. Then his arm went limp and he was no longer in control of his body, mind, or spirit. He was gone. Every animal in that temple of timber released a cry in their own species' tongue, all expressing anguish. I watched in silence as vines and branches slowly grew around the old man until he was perfectly encapsulated in a leafy chrysalis. That was where he would rest for eternity: one with the Earth.

Charlie whimpered and rested his paw on the wrapped body while Sam jumped up and assumed a perch on my shoulder. The old man's companions were in my care now. I turned back to the jaguar and it looked deep into my eyes, giving me a slow, astute blink. I took a few of my own moments to mourn the old man before finally returning to my feet. To my surprise, the once-extinct animals were patiently awaiting my reaction. A new sense of duty immediately filled the emptiness I had long carried with me. An inheritance from the father I never had. These animals needed me as much as I would come to need them.

More cherished memories of my time with the old man

filled my heart until I remembered that he left something else with me. Slowly, I raised my arm and opened my hand. A small heirloom was standing motionless in my palm. And then it hit me. The birthdays. The carvings. They were not just gifts to me, they were gifts to the world. And now I would be adding a young tiger cub to my shelf.

DESTINATION EARTH
PART III

The destination was Earth. Not their own of course, but the one that had abruptly amassed in matching orbit behind the shadow of the sun. The Goldilocks Zone, it's called.

As they soared over the alien terrain, all looked as it once did back home. Black mountain ranges, blue rivers, green valleys, open streams, dense forests, and finger-like tributaries sprawling their ways through marshy swamps. Glaciers capped the poles and deserts lined the equator and great oceans filled the voids. Abundant wildlife was seen flocking and flying and prowling and playing without heed.

The Ceres A Starship landed upright inside the safety

of a deep valley surrounded by mountains. When the white clouds of exhaust cleared, a large ramp unfolded in sections and clunked to the ground. Decompressing smoke spilled from a doorway. After a moment of quiet, out stepped thirteen individuals: two North American, two Russian, two Chinese, one African, four European, and two South American.

One by one they descended the ramp with equipment in their hands and helmets on their heads, each swiveling left and right in awe behind gold visors. Directly to their right was a circular arrangement of stones containing the white char of last night's fire. Positioned around the stones were flat log benches. This was the place.

Many of the astronauts began their experiments immediately. The Chinese were already kneeling on the ground, filling their vials with samples they dug from the earth. The Russians were helping the South Americans splay out and construct a pod-like structure. The Europeans had unfolded a large crate they had been carrying together until it displayed an advanced communication system complete with a spinning satellite. The African stood under a tree and placed a gloved hand on its bark.

The Americans pressed on.

Around a nearby outcrop that had taken seconds to form instead of centuries, the two Americans discovered an encampment not seen from their telescopes back home—thirteen identical dwellings built seamlessly into the lush terrain. Interestingly, they were advanced, but not in a technological way. Their angled roofs were an extension of the ground below, except manicured gardens grew in place of grass. The walls were an intricate combination of wood and stone that looked clever and archaic at the same time. If there were doors, they were all open inward as all they could see were the shadows of the interiors. Shadows that one human walked out from.

"Greetings, travelers," a young woman addressed. She wore a shawl of sorts, resembling cotton, with short pants underneath. Her skin was like honey and her hair dark molasses. "Welcome to Earth."

The two astronaut's helmets swiveled toward each other, then back at the mysterious woman. "Earth?" they both asked through built-in intercoms.

The woman walked delicately up to them. She had on no shoes and was humming an unknown tune. "Yes, Earth," she said.

"How is it you speak our language?" one of the astronauts asked.

The woman tilted her head in thought for a while, then simply said, "I'm not sure."

"Where did you come from?" the other astronaut asked.

This time the woman seemed distracted. She kneeled down to the ground, plucked a white clover, and handed it to the travelers. "I come from the same place as this flower."

Both parties were quiet for a time. The American

astronauts began speaking in private through their helmets while the woman just hummed and admired the landscape. "It is safe to breathe," the woman eventually said.

The helmets looked at each other once again. Everything from the mountains above to the woman standing in front of them to the white clovers below seemed exactly like that of home. The air *had* to be the same, too.

One helmet turned back to face the woman, then two gloved hands removed it. Underneath was a dark woman with thick curly hair that was happy to be released. She took a deep breath of the cleanest air she had ever breathed, and smiled. "Hello," she said, this time with an outstretched hand.

The woman before her cupped it in both of her own and shook. "Hello!"

The astronaut elbowed her partner to remove their helmet as well. "My name is May Jensen, and this is Colonel Prack."

Next to May stood an older man with a mustache and greying hair. He wedged his helmet between his torso and inner elbow and said, "Ma'am."

The woman practiced mouthing their names before replying—as if their language was mutual, but their names were alien. "It is nice to meet you May Jensen and Colonel Prack. My people call me their Didact. Come, let me introduce you."

The Didact, as light as the very air, turned on the balls of her feet and strolled back to her encampment.

"What the hell is going on here, Jensen?" Colonel Prack whispered. "Shouldn't we radio home before we mingle?"

May now realized she was half a million miles away from any sort of commanding authority. Checking in no longer seemed pressing. Besides, wasn't the scientific significance of first contact infinitely more important than protocol?

She finally shrugged, said, "This is just as new for me as it is for you," then started following their ebullient host.

Colonel Prack was stuck. His whole professional life was in the service of his country and its citizens. He was proud of it; defined by it. But even he had to admit that no harm was met from this new planet and its greeter.

When the colonel caught up, the other eleven astronauts had rounded the outcrop and were welcomed warmly by the Didact as well. May was introduced to the one they called their scientist and was already deep in questioning. The other eleven of her council, as the Didact called them, were just as friendly and gracious as herself, and were happy to give the travelers a tour of their humble encampment.

The garden-like roofs of their homes, they explained, were angled so the plants requiring the most amount of sun and the least amount of water were at the top, while those requiring the most amount of water and the least amount of sun were at the bottom. The rock and wood walls were engineered to insulate, yet still allow airflow for cooling, maintaining a consistent temperature year round. They also had tools to dig wells and stones to grind metal and carts to carry loads. Nothing more wanted, nothing more wasted.

When the afternoon sun hung low, the astronauts began sharing their own world with the scientist and the council. They talked about their nations and languages and demonstrated the technology they brought with. The scientist was fascinated by the European's communication radio while the council was enthralled by their words and ways. May was standing back, admiring the way in which twenty-six people—half strangers to the other half—could learn and discover and work together so harmoniously, when she felt a hand on her shoulder.

"May Jensen?" It was the Didact. She had a new look in her eyes. One that projected gravity. "Would you come with me for a moment?"

May nodded, picked up her helmet, and followed. No one seemed to notice.

The Didact led May through a grove of coniferous trees to a nearby river. It was wide and lively and clear as crystal, maybe clearer. On their side of the shore stood a small mill automated by the water's flow. Across the way looked to be an unfinished turbine, perhaps in the early stages of harnessing renewable electricity. Further downriver a pack of large elk had gathered for an evening drink. But behind the elk, and far beyond the white-capped mountains, sat something so enormous, so paramount to May's entire understanding of existence, that it weakened her knees just to lay eyes upon.

Her first Earthset.

"Come," the Didact said, then entered the transparent water with bare feet. She stepped lightly until she reached a small island that forced the lively river around it.

Nearly unable to peel her eyes away from her home, May trudged through the water in her spacesuit, muddling the transparency with white splashes. A fish had decided it intrusive and leapt through the air.

Together on the island they stood and watched the setting Earth. The mirror image looming in the stars was statistically impossible—an incalculable reflection cast on a cosmic scale. Monumental in meaning. Both planets shared the same elements, the same sun, the same moon, and the same orbit, yet neither had disturbed the other...until today.

"I sense that great strife has followed you here, May Jensen," the Didact eventually said.

May was taken aback. Sure tensions on Earth had grown thick while alliances wore thin, but five continents banded together to bring the Ceres project to life. It was a symbol of hope, of solidarity. A reminder that all of humanity still had one thing in common: curiosity. "What do you mean?"

"I can see fear in your council's eyes, hear uncertainty in their voices."

May furrowed her brow. "*My* council? No, we're just—"

"They are afraid they will lose everything. They will turn to you when they are lost."

"What's going to happen? How can you know this?"

The Didact faced May, and May faced the Didact. They looked into each other with disquieted eyes. The Didact frowned.

"I have no memories of my life from before, May Jensen. I have only feelings that return to me in my sleep. I have dreams of dangerous caves, of quakes and darkness. I have dreams of a mighty sphere and of blinding light. In these dreams I see twelve pairs of desperate eyes begging me for an answer I cannot give, but then I wake up here. And I am happy."

May did not understand entirely what the Didact was trying to say, but she wanted to listen.

"There was a great suffering with my people. I know there was no choice but to leave. I know we are all that is left. And this...this beautiful Earth...she saved us...and we saved her. This is what I know."

May, tears welling in her eyes, watched the Didact's kind gaze fall to the ground. Science aside, she believed the Didact when she spoke of her past. Perhaps there was a mighty sphere that transported their Earth across the cosmos to orbit the sun in tandem with her own. It would not be the most unbelievable thing she had seen this last year.

May wrapped her hand around the Didact's arm and gave it a gentle squeeze. "I'm so sorry."

Just then, static permeated from the intercom inside May's helmet. The Europeans must have made contact with their own Earth. She released the Didact's arm to retrieve it from the ground and held it up to both of their ears.

Shhhhck...

Fifty warships have been spotted off the coast of...

Shhhhck...

Troops are deploying across the continent...

Shhhhck...

Mass panic as citizens flee from...

Shhhhck...

Pings are flashing all over the map...

Shhhhck...

Air Force One has been shot down...

Shhhhck...

There is no response from the President...

Shhhhck...

My God. What have we done?...

Shhhhhhhhck...

The helmet dropped to the rocky isle with a sharp thunk. Both May and the Didact looked outwards at the setting Earth. A single pop of light appeared on its surface. Followed by another. Then another. Then another. All barely seen with the naked eye, but each unmistakable. In their wake, mushroom shaped clouds bloomed outward like entrails of extinction.

May placed a trembling hand on her mouth, tears streaming down her cheeks. It was true she and Colonel Prack had left Earth in conflict, but she had also left with the hope that this expedition would unite its nations; the same hope she had felt when she spotted a brand new planet through her telescope.

Empty minutes went by in silence when May suddenly felt something in her other hand. It was the warmth and comfort of interlaced fingers.

"I am sorry, May Jensen," the Didact said. "Tomorrow will be better."

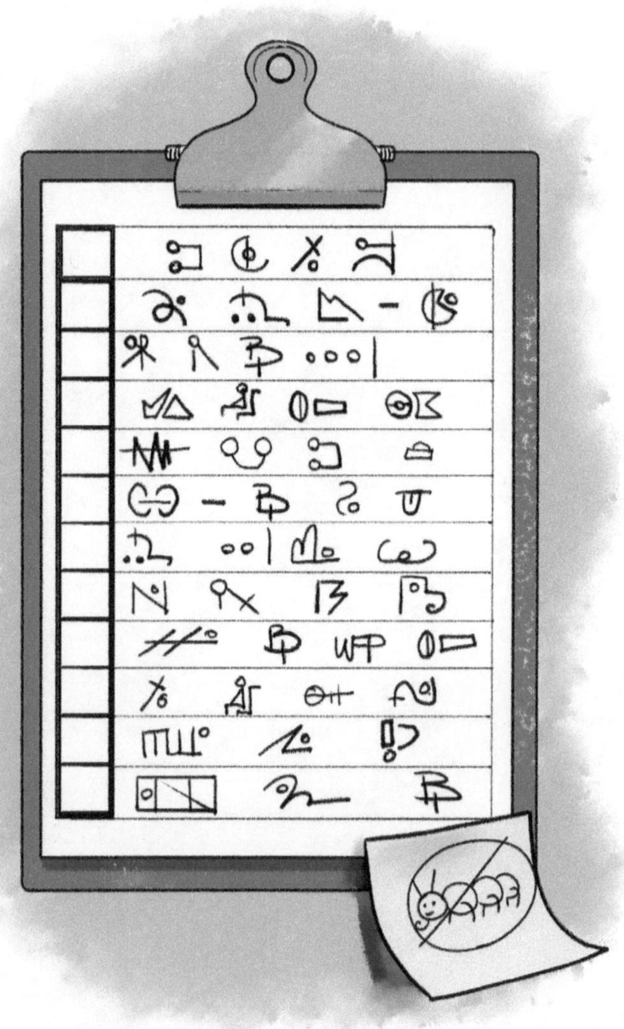

LOST VEGAS

AN EPILOGUE OF SORTS

In the years following the Collapse, the sky eventually became less yellow, less cancerous. The flat sheet of fallout had dissipated and allowed the sun to stimulate the ground once again. With the return of vegetation came the expected return of insects. With the return of insects came the return of reptiles, birds, and small mammals. Following them was the return of healthy diurnal and nocturnal ecosystems. And with all of this return came a returning interest in Earth.

Out of the cloudless desert sky over what was once southern Nevada, a large orb of unmathematical explanation soared south until touching down on a black strip of shattered concrete. There it hovered for a while—silent, steady—completely undisturbed and completely undisturbing.

After a time, a bright ring traced itself out of the precise axial bottom of the orb, creating a platform that lowered slowly to the ground. Atop the platform were two beings holding standard issue clipboards.

"Last one," Tarzip said as her tendrils flipped through the clipped pages.

Grild stepped off the platform first. His soft, voidish flesh singed on the street so he pressed a button attached to his suit that enveloped him in a non-evaporating liquid. "About time. I was starting to think we'd never get through them all."

Tarzip, scent hole catching a waft of Grild's fried skin, tapped her button first before joining him on the scorched earth. She then manifested a floating disk in her hand that projected some figures in the air. "Interesting," she mused.

"What?" Grild commented, though his focus was now on the white-hot sun above. The liquid near his many eyes had darkened so he could gaze upon Sol safely.

"The Companion says we are in the right spot..." She paused for a moment, looked outward, and considered the city that surrounded them. " . . . but I don't see any signs."

"It's possible none survived the blast," Grild said while he took a pen from his pocket and clicked the actuator. "I say we trust the Companion and Reset this place so we can go home."

Tarzip furrowed what could be considered a brow. "No. Article two-ninety-seven of the Galactic Association of Certified Planet Inspectors' bylaws requires us to confirm a city's identity before Reset. You remember what happened last time, don't you?"

"Yeah, yeah," Grild sighed.

The two left the orb in park and began their hunt for evidence in the city they now occupied. At first glance it looked much like all of the other ruined cities they had Reset that day—roughly two hundred and seventy Earth hours to them—and they did not yet see anything worth being checked off on their checklists. Fallen billboards here, crumpled marquees there, all of them bleached white by stinging radiation and unfiltered sunlight. Common sights in their line of work.

"So," Grild brought up to break the long silence forming at the end of a long day, "do you know anything about the seller?"

One of Tarzip's stalk eyes glared at her coworker while the others continued to monitor her surroundings. "Not much," she replied, "but I heard on their last visit they lost some sort of game to an Earth child."

All of Grild's eyes blinked in unison. "An Earth *child*? I don't believe that for a second."

Tarzip smirked. "It's just what I heard."

They walked quietly for a while longer, Tarzip occasionally checking her Companion and Grild clicking his pen. Frustration was on the cusp of setting in when Tarzip noticed something in the near distance and pointed at it with a single tendril. "Hold up, what's that?"

"What's what?"

"*That!*" Tarzip pointed harder. "I swear I've seen it before."

Grild's many eyes suddenly plunged themselves into one big eye that adjusted its focus in and out to see the distant object clearer. "Oh, yeah! That was uh..."

Tarzip spoke some words into her Companion until it projected the exact object she was referring to. "The Eiffel Tower! From the Earth city once called Paris."

"Right, right," Grild said, returning his optics to normal. "Didn't we already Reset that?"

"Yet here it stands."

———

A short walk later and both of them stood directly beneath the tower that they were certain they had Reset earlier in their shift.

"Why would humans waste their waning resources building a copy that's less than half the original's size?" Grild thought aloud, then ticked the checkbox on his clipboard marked *gratuitous*.

Tarzip was about to reply with another question when just behind them a loud whooshing and splashing interrupted her train of thought. Her stalk eyes flicked backwards to witness jets of water spraying hundreds of Earth-feet into the air. Auricle-splitting sound followed in unison.

Underneath the liquid lining of Grild's suit his void skin began to warp. He rippled while shouting at Tarzip. "Is this what humans call music!"

"I don't know!" Tarzip yelled back. She quickly manifested her Companion again, gave it an order, and it zipped off into the distance. Moments later there was a loud *zap!* and the music and fountain died immediately.

When the waves stopped on Grild's skin, he looked at his clipboard and checked off *grandeur* and *cacophony*. "What an absurd way to display precious drinking water when living in an arid climate."

"Perhaps it's some ritual flaunting of excess," Tarzip added. "This was a wealthy nation."

"Excess?" Grild sounded offended. "On our way in I noticed the entire river feeding the nearby lake was nothing but sand. By all accounts, this city probably shouldn't have existed in the first place!"

"That may be so, but we still need some sort of sign to confirm it for Reset. Let's keep looking."

Grild mumbled, then ticked off *improvident* as well.

———

Their search for something resembling a sign lasted them

deep into the afternoon. The sky began to cool and the two inspectors could safely deactivate their liquid suits.

They had decided to split up and work their way south—according to Earth's magnetism—and eventually Tarzip met up with Grild outside of a museum that actually had an intact sign, though not the one they were seeking.

"The Extraordinary Expedition of Worldly Explanations? Really?" she mocked, looking up at a neon-outlined human crudely animated in a way that made it look like it was falling.

"It's actually quite charming," Grild explained, now donning a human hat that read *Property of W.G.* on the front. "It seems some nineteenth-century explorer believed that an ancient civilization had dug a hole through the center of this planet."

Tarzip rolled her stalk eyes. "Which would certainly void its warranty."

"True," Grild agreed, then ticked *destructive*.

"Now, let's keep looking for our sign. It's nearly dark out."

But just as Tarzip mentioned the waning light, a glow that rivaled the sun itself exploded behind Grild, leaving only the black silhouette of his body. Grild turned and they both stood in awe at the dead, unnamed city in the desert.

One-by-one every building illuminated, morphing night into midday. Attractions began to whir and clack and move and striplighting brightly guided their circular and linear paths. The Eiffel Tower replica along with an entire copy of

New York—another city they had Reset earlier—reached for the sky with pulsating brilliance. Backlit, weathered signs glowed with the empty promise of amusements from the past. The city was alive.

"Woah," Grild said unexpectedly.

"Woah indeed," Tarzip agreed.

"This violates every single ecological and environmental law in the Intergalactic Planetary Preservation Act, but somehow I don't mind."

They both stood and watched the city entertain itself without the need of a population. A giant wheel turned, a cart attached to some sort of railing looped in and out of a building, music burst from every perceivable orifice. All of that power, all of that splendor, exuberated for absolutely no one other than the desert night.

"Hey, Grild," Tarzip said, nudging his side.

"What?" he asked, peeling his gaze away from the city enough to notice Tarzip was facing the other direction.

"Look!"

Due to the brightness, all of Grild's eyes had nearly retreated into his head. He forced them back out and lumped them together again to make out a distant object. "Could it be?"

Both of them summoned their Companions, which grew in size and sprouted a handle that they could grip. When they hopped on, each Companion took off down the illuminated road until they reached a bright sign standing tall on a partition between themselves and the next road over. Strangely, its message had not faded.

"Drive carefully, come back soon?" Grild read aloud, hopping off of his Companion while looking upwards. "That's not on our list."

But Tarzip was already on the other side, smirking at what she had read. "Get over here, you big lump."

Grild walked around and joined her line of sight. He could not help but smirk as well. Above them read "Welcome to Fabulous Las Vegas," but the "Las" had been replaced with someone's clever rendition of the word "Lost".

"It's a shame," Tarzip eventually said, "They inevitably destroyed themselves by maintaining this type of lifestyle all around the globe. But even in their absence, you can't say they didn't have a sense of humor."

Grild checked the final box on his clipboard reading *narcissistic*. "No, no you cannot."

———

When Tarzip and Grild had returned to the orb and lifted off, they looked down at the shining city from their viewing platform, almost in admiration. Then, after the briefest moment of hesitation, Tarzip used her tendrils to initiate the Reset.

Beneath them the bright lights and the loud sounds sucked inwards until suddenly the desert sat vacant in darkness. It was as if humanity had never been there in the first place, never built a city of neon, of lights. Everything that had ever happened in Las Vegas would stay in Las Vegas only as memory. There would be no second chances. It was gone forever.

Lost.

THANK YOU

Wow, thank YOU for reading *Destination Earth*! Whether you're still recovering from *Man, Kind,* or this is your first experience with my work, I sincerely appreciate the valuable time you gave to my stories.

If I could trouble you for just five more minutes, please leave an honest rating and/or review on Goodreads, Amazon, or wherever you purchased this book from. The only way my work stands out from the mainstream is if it has those little yellow stars under the title. A sincere thank you from myself and all other independent authors.

And finally, an essential list of thank yous. Thanks to Brent, my friend and illustrator, for going way above and beyond what this project initially called for. Thank you to my editors, Heidi (my mom) and Lily (my sister), for digging into each story and pointing out all of my missteps. Thanks to NayNay for making the epic companion video and to Bryo for composing an original jam. Thank you to my wife, Abby, who tolerates my silly ideas and helps with literally everything I do creatively. And thank you to all of the friends and family and fans who have ever sent me an encouraging message; you're the proverbial ink in my pen.

ILLUSTRATOR

Much to the chagrin of his mother, Brent Plooster is an artist, illustrator, and musician from Sioux Falls, SD. Brent is the proud father of four wonderful kids: AJ (19), Brayden (15), Everley (8) and William (1) and husband to Maggie. Most days, you can find him playing video games, Dungeon Mastering for his kids, and inexplicably watching lawn care videos on YouTube. Stop by www.brentiisdesign.com to say hi, see his body of work, or invite him to join your D&D campaign.

```
Ioprq: R sjdk yju R wjudk nrgk c wcy sj orke c
feqqcte rg yjup hjjb. Socgb yju njp cddjwrgt fe
sj he lcps jn sorq ajupgey. R cllpeircse yjup
npregkqorl, cgk djve sorq hjjb

Fcttre : Socgb yju njp yjup ugwcveprgt qulljps.
R ijudkg's ocve kjge sorq wrsojus yju. R djve
yju fjpe socg cgysorgt. Djve, Hpegs
```

ÅUTHOR

Chris (C.C.) Berke is the award-winning author of *Man, Kind* and a chronic daydreamer. He has spent most of his life in South Dakota, but has a deep fondness for traveling, especially to the Rocky Mountains of Colorado. When he's not reading or writing, he enjoys spending time with his supportive wife, Abby, and his two cats, Henry and Winston. You may also encounter him in *Destiny 2* under the guise of ccberke_author.

Destination Earth is his second novel.

A FINAL NOTE

When people say "shop local", it's more than just a turn of phrase for me. Supporting local (or independent) authors, artists, and creators is by far the best way to discover something truly unique. Something no one else in any other region could ever offer.

In a couple of the stories from this collection I mention South Dakota, my home state. Sure, those narratives could have taken place anywhere, but would they have the same impact coming from me; have the same impact on you? Maybe you've been to Falls Park in Sioux Falls and you've walked by the remains of the Queen Bee Mill. Now, *The Mother's Eye* means a little bit more to you because you've experienced where it came from.

So that's why I am launching more than just *Destination Earth* on www.sodakpublishing.com. I have also created the *Definitive Guide To Self Publishing*: a step-by-step tutorial that covers all aspects of the industry. It's completely free to any and all dreamers who want to publish a book of their own in a beautiful and professional manner.

And this is only the beginning . . .

ACCESS GRANTED

For more great stories and a full guide to self-publishing, please visit www.sodakpublishing.com!

ARCHIVE

FIGURE 1
destination earth: part I

FIGURE 2
the traveler

FIGURE 3
the last drop

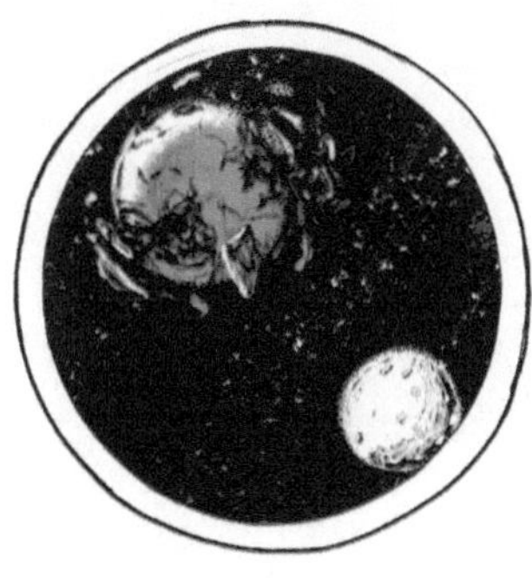

FIGURE 4
destination earth: part II